NO PLACE TO VANISH

(MURDER IN THE KEYS: BOOK #2)

JADEN SKYE

Books by Jaden Skye

THE CARIBBEAN MURDER SERIES
DEATH BY HONEYMOON (Book #1)
DEATH BY DIVORCE (Book #2)
DEATH BY MARRIAGE (Book #3)
DEATH BY DESIRE (Book #4)
DEATH BY DECEIT (Book #5)
DEATH BY JEALOUSY (Book #6)
DEATH BY PROPOSAL (Book #7)
DEATH BY OBSESSION (Book #8)
DEATH BY DEVOTION (Book #9)
DEATH BY BETRAYAL (Book #10)
DEATH BY REQUEST (Book #11)
DEATH BY ENGAGEMENT (Book #12)
DEATH BY SEDUCTION (Book #13)
DEATH BY TEMPTATION (Book #14)
DEATH BY INVITATION (Book #15)
DEATH BY WEDDING (Book #16)

THE TOM'S RIVER SAGA
A PERFECT STRANGER (Book #1)

MURDER IN THE KEYS
NO PLACE TO DIE (Book #1)
NO PLACE TO VANISH (Book #2)

THE KILLING GAME
INVITATION TO DIE (Book #1)
INVITATION TO MADNESS (Book #2)
INVITATION TO AGONY (Book #3)

Jacket image Copyright mrfiza and By I_B, used under license from shuitterstock.

ISBN: 978-1-64029-126-3

CHAPTER ONE

As the plane tossed through the gathering clouds, Olivia looked out the window, replaying all that had gone on. It was still impossible to believe that she was returning to New York alone. Todd wasn't with her; he was gone. Her hand reached out to the empty seat beside her as her mind continued to play games. He'll be back in a minute, her mind whispered. This was all a dream, Todd's alive, he's well. He'll be there at the airport waiting when you arrive.

Of course Olivia knew that Todd wouldn't be there, not today, nor ever again. It was hard to believe that they'd gotten engaged in Key West only a few weeks ago. The engagement ring Todd had given Olivia right before he was killed still sat on her finger, looking up at her, gleaming. At times it was soothing to look at it, reminding her of wonderful times. Other times the ring seemed to be mocking her, daring her to take it off, put it in a drawer, and move on.

The plane took a sudden dip in the growing turbulence that accompanied the flight. Images of Todd on his death bed, struggling to breathe, flashed through Olivia's mind. She recalled sitting alone in the emergency room, late at night, waiting for a word of hope. Her first encounter with Todd's disturbing family came to her vividly, how they'd adamantly refused to believe that Olivia and Todd had become engaged.

Olivia listened to the rain falling on the plane as an airline stewardess suddenly leaned toward her.

"Can I get you anything at all?" she asked.

Olivia looked up at her sadly.

Bring Todd back to me, she wanted to say, but forced herself to smile instead.

"Thank you very much, but not now," Olivia replied.

Since the crime had been solved, and Todd's former girlfriend, Rhonda, convicted, Olivia hadn't been able to sleep or eat much. During the few weeks of investigation, wave after wave of shock and horror kept occurring, almost daily. Olivia not only met the disturbing people in Todd's life, but one sordid fact after another about him became revealed. To top it off, Olivia discovered that he was still sleeping with his ex-girlfriend Rhonda, even as she and Todd were becoming engaged. She knew she should hate Todd now.

But for some reason, she still loved him.

1

Olivia knew that, without her uncanny insight and courage, Rhonda would have gone free. Yet, despite all the attention and adulation Olivia received at the end, she took little pleasure in it. The future lay spread out before her now—and she had no idea what was in store.

*

When the plane finally landed back in New York, a row of cabs were lined up outside the airport. Olivia got her bags quickly and took one of the cabs to her upscale apartment, on a fashionable street in the Upper East Side, overlooking the river.

As soon as the cab pulled up to her building, a doorman, Russo, came out and helped bring her things in. In a daze Olivia slowly followed him inside and gazed around the lobby. All kinds of perfectly dressed people were coming and going as they always did, looking confident and secure. It was as if their carefully constructed worlds were built on a solid foundation and couldn't fall apart in a second, as Olivia's just had.

"Good to have you back home again," Russo commented lightly as they got into the elevator and pressed a high floor.

"Thanks so much," Olivia replied, as the elevator lifted up quickly. Of course Russo meant well, but it saddened Olivia to be welcomed home. Even though she and Todd hadn't actually lived together, he'd spent most nights here with her since they met. They'd been inseparable. Now, without him, her place didn't feel like home anymore.

Russo brought her bags into the apartment, piled them carefully next to one another, wished her well, and left.

Olivia then began to wander aimlessly through the beautifully decorated rooms. Todd's things were still scattered around here and there, including a few photos of them together, smiling. In the photos it looked as if the entire world had belonged to them. Olivia could not bring herself to look at the photos closely. She also could not imagine taking them down. The time would come when she could, she thought. But for now, she felt lost and confused, wondering if things would ever normalize again.

Olivia walked over to one of the large glass windows, pulled up the blinds, and leaned against the dusty windowpane. Standing up here high on top of the world, she looked out at the river, where tugboats passed along just as before. Olivia remembered how much she and Todd used to enjoy walking at the river's edge at the end of the day. She also thought of his texts and emails that she'd so enjoyed receiving. How they talked almost all night long, curled up in each other's arms. Olivia's life had totally changed the moment they'd met. Todd said his had, too.

Now, she had no idea what to believe anymore.

The phone rang sharply, but Olivia didn't even try to answer. She couldn't. Not yet. It was too soon to talk to friends, put on a cheerful face, and pretend that she was the same person she'd been when she left a few weeks ago. Perhaps she just needed to settle in and after a bath and good dinner, she'd feel more like herself.

No, she needed more than that.

She knew that tomorrow morning she needed to get up and go back to work, full steam ahead. To immerse herself back in her old life. Otherwise, she would just waste away here, wallow away in misery and depression. And that wasn't an option.

Somehow, she had to find a way to pick up the pieces and move on.

Yet, she just didn't know if she could do it.

CHAPTER TWO

Olivia barely slept all night, just tossed in the midst of rocky dreams. At times she felt as if Todd were with her again. Other times she dreamt she was back with her first fiancé, Paul. In her dream she was sitting at Paul's bedside in the long vigil his sickness took them through. Paul was begging her to stay beside him.

Olivia awoke harshly at the crack of dawn, breathing hard, rubbing her eyes. Both Paul and Todd were gone now. It was time to face the new day alone. Like Todd, Paul had also died before they could marry, a couple of years ago. Olivia's experience with Paul was entirely different though. He'd died after a long battle with cancer. He wasn't horribly poisoned by a vengeful girlfriend as Todd had been. And layers of deceit, fraud, and scandal hadn't been exposed about Paul.

After Paul died, it had taken a long while to regroup. Olivia didn't want to go through that again now with Todd. She didn't have the time or energy to do so. And most importantly, she didn't want to. Did Todd deserve it, even? He'd lied to her, played her for a fool. What Olivia had learned about him after his death had thrust her into deep confusion about her own judgment. Why hadn't she seen any of the truth of what was going on? How could she have been so blind?

Olivia jumped out of bed and went straight to the bathroom to shower and dress. She was determined to leave these memories behind and go forward. She was back in the city now and it was time for things to turn around.

The cool water in the shower was refreshing, woke her fully up. Olivia stood there a long time as the water poured down, hoping it would wash away the pain and horror. She grabbed a loofah brush and scrubbed her body hard, wanting to remove the grit and pain. Whether she wanted to or not, it was time to get ready for a new beginning again.

Finally, she turned off the shower, got out, dried herself briskly, and put on a crisp, beige linen suit. Then she brushed her long, beautiful, blonde hair over and over, hoping to return to her normally pristine self.

Acting as if nothing were different today, Olivia went into the kitchen and made a quick pot of coffee, scrambled some eggs, and popped a few pieces of whole wheat bread into the toaster. She knew that the sooner she could create a semblance of her old routine, the better she would feel.

4

After eating breakfast and cleaning the dishes, she decided to get into the office as soon as she could. Earlier would be better. She'd throw herself fully back into the work she'd loved as a book publicist for a top publishing company. The work had always been rewarding and exciting and Olivia hoped it would continue to be so.

Ready to leave, Olivia grabbed her briefcase and headed straight for the door. She'd get to the office, see her colleagues, and take care of whatever was there waiting for her.

*

Olivia's company was located midtown on the twenty-fifth floor, overlooking a busy avenue with cars, buses, and trucks honking on top of each other, all day long. Her office, which faced the street, was small but bright, with a large desk in the center strewn with papers. A sizable bookcase covered the far wall. The bookcase was filled with books on display that Olivia had worked on, proudly.

As soon as she walked in, it was as if no time had passed and those horrible weeks in Key West were entirely unreal. No one was in the office yet and Olivia slipped behind her desk quickly. First thing, she would sort out the piles of papers that were on it. As she picked up one paper after another and started to read, her eyes began to blur. It was hard to focus on the words in front of her. Her mind kept returning to Todd.

Olivia knew that colleagues and clients would soon be arriving and were expecting to see her today. The idea of seeing everyone suddenly filled her with dread. Would they be sorry for her and treat her gingerly? Would they see her as a two-time loser? Or would they be distant and nervous in the face of the tragedy she'd just been through? Either way was distasteful. Olivia felt unnerved.

She quickly flipped open her computer to scroll through emails and go over an old assignment she'd been working on. Once again, the words just flashed before her eyes. Try as she might, she couldn't concentrate. Or, when she finally did, whatever she read seemed completely meaningless now.

Olivia closed her eyes and tried again, but the same thing happened. She couldn't do it! Her attention had been taken over. Her heart and soul were no longer here. A big part of her was still down in Key West and she was having trouble bringing it back so soon. To Olivia's dismay, she then began sobbing. She got up, went to the window, and looked down at the bustling traffic and pedestrians trying to cross the streets. She wasn't ready for this by a long shot. She had returned to the office way too soon.

Grateful that no one was here yet, Olivia grabbed her briefcase and made for the door. She needed more time badly. How long? She had no idea. She'd go home, write to her boss, and ask for her leave of absence to be extended.

Indefinitely.

*

It was even hard returning to her apartment now. Once inside, Olivia quickly sent an email to the office explaining that she wasn't ready to return, asking for more time.

How much time? came the quick reply. *We were surprised not to see you here today.*

Not really sure, Olivia answered truthfully. *I'll let you know soon, though.*

Olivia then thought about texting Allison, whom she used to confide in regularly. But there was nothing in particular to confide and truthfully, Olivia didn't want to hear anything Allison had to say. She needed something entirely different now, she realized.

Her phone suddenly rang. Undoubtedly, it was someone from the office. Olivia knew she had to pick up.

"Olivia Wells?" a strange male voice answered, surprising her.

"Yes?" asked Olivia, wondering who it was.

"I realize there's no way you can recognize my voice," he continued. "But it's Sean Merkin, Raine's husband."

Olivia was confused. Raine had been her best friend in college, though they'd lost touch over the past few years. When Olivia hadn't attended her wedding, Raine had distanced herself. Olivia explained she had to be out of the country, that the trip had been planned for almost a year. But Raine wouldn't listen. It was startling to hear from Raine's husband, Sean, now.

"Of course I know who you are. How are you?" Olivia quickly replied.

"I've been better." Sean's voice lowered.

"Is everything all right?" Olivia had no idea why he was calling now.

"I'm sure it's all fine." Sean started talking quickly. "And I know it's crazy to call, but I heard how instrumental you were in solving a case in Key West and I was impressed."

"Thank you," said Olivia, startled. It was actually comforting to be speaking to him.

6

"Raine heard about it too, and she was fascinated," Sean quickly added.

"How is Raine?" Olivia immediately picked up on it.

"That's what I'm calling about." Sean's voice grew husky.

Olivia had a moment of fear that Raine was ill. Was he calling on her behalf? Did Raine need something from her now?

"Raine recently went down to Key West to be at a friend's bachelorette party," Sean continued. "She was supposed to come back two days ago."

"Yes?" Olivia was not clear about where he was headed.

"She still hasn't returned," Sean announced.

"I'm not exactly understanding," Olivia remarked.

"Raine was due home two days ago," Sean repeated, nervously. "We live in Miami, a short trip away."

"Raine's probably with one of her friends," Olivia commented, not knowing what Sean had in mind.

"She's not," Sean answered briskly. "I've spoken to them. They all know each other, most live in Miami, nearby. Her friend Pietra organized the party, and Raine's mom came here to take care of Clea while she was gone."

"Clea?" Olivia was startled.

"We have a one-year-old little girl," Sean mumbled.

"No one told me." Olivia felt sad.

"Sorry about that," Sean conceded. "There was so much going on when the baby was born. Anyway, you don't happen to know Pietra, who organized the party, do you?"

"No," said Olivia. She didn't know any of the new friends Raine had made living in Florida, or anything else about her life. "Raine and I lost touch."

"I know that you did." Sean sounded disconcerted. "Raine talked about it from time to time. I actually told her to call you when we heard about Todd's death. But Raine felt funny about it."

Olivia cringed. "I'm sorry to hear that," she replied.

"Listen, right now I'm nervous," Sean repeated loudly. "I'm still waiting for Raine to come home. She's not answering her texts, phone, or emails, either."

Suddenly, it hit Olivia. "Are you saying Raine's missing?" she asked in horror.

"I'm not saying that," Sean responded. "I'm just saying she's not yet home!"

"Which of her friends have you talked to?" Olivia picked right up on it. "Did she travel down to Key West with any of them?"

Sean's voice grew edgy. "Raine actually went down earlier, a day before the party. As far as I know she was planning to stay a few hours extra after they were and fly back alone. The gals all tell me not to worry, that everything's fine. Most think she's just giving herself a few days off the grid. Raine likes going off the grid from time to time."

Olivia felt better hearing that, but still uneasy. "Doesn't Raine usually tell you when she's going off the grid?"

"Yes, she does." Sean breathed hard. "And with each hour that's passing, I'm feeling worse."

"Of course you are," Olivia responded, now fully engaged.

"In fact, I'm freaking out, if you really want the truth," he blurted out.

"I do really want the truth," Olivia responded intensely.

"I thought you would." Sean sounded somber. "I'm scared something awful's happened to Raine, and I need someone on this with me. You did such a great job finding Todd's killer. Please, will you come down and help? I'll pay for your trip, your time, for everything."

Olivia was shocked by the request and also completely mobilized. The idea of helping out excited her. And it would be wonderful to see Raine again as well. Without a moment's hesitation she made up her mind.

"I'll be on the first flight tomorrow, Sean," she said.

"You will? Really?" He seemed thrilled.

"Yes, I will," said Olivia. "See you then."

CHAPTER THREE

Olivia was relieved to be leaving the city and it was good being back on an early flight first thing the next morning. Looking out the window in the plane, Olivia drank one cup of coffee after another. What would it be like to see Raine again? Olivia was eager to meet Sean again and see Raine's daughter. Olivia was shocked to realize that Raine had a child and hadn't told her. That wasn't like her. It wasn't the sparkly, fun-loving Raine Olivia remembered from college, who was always up for anything and made everyone laugh.

Before Raine and Olivia were roommates at college, they'd become best friends. Raine majored in visual arts, with a specialty in photography, and had posted her photographs all over their room. Raine loved taking photographs of everything she'd laid her eyes on. She had a hunger for life, always went where it took her. Olivia was always more naturally cautious, but greatly enjoyed Raine's spirit of adventure. Raine enjoyed Olivia's practical side and her ability to balance things out.

As Olivia thought about Raine's life now, complete with a husband and young daughter, it was startling to realize that she herself was still single and alone.

The voice of the pilot over the loudspeaker suddenly interrupted Olivia's reverie, announcing that it was time to prepare for landing. They would be arriving early, before the expected time.

*

Back in a cab once again, now leaving the Miami airport, Olivia headed toward Raine's home. It was located in an established, upscale suburb of Miami, not exactly the kind of life Olivia would have imagined for Raine. Olivia would have thought she would be living in the midst of a city, exploring every nook and cranny, shopping, partying, and drinking coffee in outdoor cafes, even in the rain.

As the cab drew closer to the destination, Olivia tried her best to remember Sean. She'd only met him a few times briefly. He and Raine had just met at the end of senior year. Sean had attended a proper all-male school a few miles away and he and Raine had met at a year-end mixer. Olivia recalled that Sean had seemed older than his years, handsome, formal, and determined. He also wouldn't leave Raine alone, pursued her for all he was worth. Raine had been flattered by the attention but Olivia remembered wondering if he was right for her. Sean was different from the guys Raine usually dated, stiffer and more demanding.

After graduation, Olivia moved home to Boston, and Raine moved to Chicago to be near Sean. After that, Olivia and Raine saw each other only occasionally. They communicated mostly through email and phone, but soon Raine became harder and harder to reach, always very busy, swooped up by Sean.

The cab left the main highway now and drove along the opulent, beautifully manicured streets. They passed one large, imposing stucco home after another with outdoor porches and verandas. Old trees and plants bloomed everywhere. The neighborhood was clearly for the well-heeled, those who lived orderly, sumptuous lives.

The cab drove Olivia to one of the most beautiful homes at the end of a flowering cul-de-sac.

"This is it," the driver said, as he pulled up.

Olivia paid him and got out of the cab slowly. Was Raine back home yet? she wondered. Any word from her at all? Although Olivia secretly hoped to find Raine waiting there, she realized that Sean would probably have let her know if she'd returned.

The moment Olivia rang the front doorbell, it opened. A tall, attractive man in his mid-thirties, wearing khakis and an open blue shirt, stood there. It was definitely Sean, looking the same as when Olivia had seen him years ago, just older. He and Olivia looked at each other directly.

"You got here fast, thank you for that. Truly. Come in," said Sean.

"No word of anything yet?" Olivia asked as she followed him into the large, open, sunny, beautiful home.

"Nothing, nothing," he muttered, running his hands through his sandy hair.

Olivia was torn between wanting to calm him down and questioning him about every detail he could remember.

"Come sit down in the living room," Sean directed. "I'll have May bring you coffee and sandwiches."

"Is that Raine's mother?" asked Olivia.

Sean's face briefly soured. "No, May is the housekeeper. Raine's mother, Barna, is out walking with Clea. They'll be back in a little while. You must have met Raine's mother at one time or another?"

"Yes, of course," Olivia replied, although it had been only briefly, in passing. Raine and her mother had never been close. It often took days before Raine even answered her calls.

"Barna's been very good to us since Clea was born." Sean quickly filled Olivia in. "She's wonderful with the baby, too. And Clea loves her."

"That's good." Olivia was glad to hear it, and also looking forward to meeting the child.

"Sit down," Sean directed her again, "I'll tell May you've arrived. We've all been expecting you. I told Raine's friends you were coming, as well."

Olivia sat down on the dark blue velvet sofa and wondered what was coming next. It was strange being here, but felt right as well. Certainly, much better than being cooped up in an office or in her apartment in the city. Olivia wondered how Raine would react to seeing her when she returned.

Sean returned quickly with May, a beautiful, slender Philippine young woman, who smiled at Olivia as she handed her a tray with coffee, salad, and an egg salad sandwich.

"Thanks so much," said Olivia, though she wasn't at all hungry.

"It's good of you to help, very good," said May. "We're all waiting for Miss Raine to come home." Then she nodded at Sean and quickly skirted away.

Sean sat opposite Olivia as she ate a few bites of the lunch, watching her carefully. "Sorry about what happened with you and Raine," he finally said as she put her sandwich back down on the tray. "She always spoke highly of you, felt bad about your friendship dissolving the way it did."

"It happens." Olivia nodded.

"Looks like you've had quite a life though," Sean went on.

Olivia wasn't exactly sure how to take that. "It's been challenging," she replied.

"You've become strong from it, Olivia, I saw that right away," Sean replied. "And from what the news reported, you basically solved Todd's case single-handedly."

Olivia had never thought of it that way. "The police worked hard on it as well," she replied, wondering why Sean hadn't contacted the police himself by now.

"Have you contacted the police about Raine?" she decided to ask.

Sean shuddered. "No, of course not. Not yet."

"Time's of the essence in the case of missing persons though," Olivia commented.

"And what if Raine just walks in the door?" Sean exclaimed. "If I contacted the police and word got out, it would upset our entire community. Raine and I are pillars of the community here, you know. We organize charity events, church attendance, bible studies, caring for the poor."

Olivia had had no idea of that. She could not recall Raine ever doing that before.

"I've told Raine over and over that this is the right way to live," Sean filled Olivia in.

"Very admirable," Olivia murmured.

"Listen, I want you to speak to all her friends," he went on. "One of them has to know what's going on. Raine can play crazy games at times, you know that. It's fun for her."

Olivia did remember that Raine could be mischievous, enjoyed pranks and surprises. This was way more than a foolish prank, though. Or was it? Olivia needed some background immediately.

"How do you guys do together?" she asked. "What's your relationship like?"

Sean got up and started pacing. "Of course I knew sooner or later you would ask that," he replied. "It's wonderful. It always was and always will be. Right from the moment we met we were happy."

Olivia took a deep breath. She'd just said and thought the very same thing herself about Todd. Actually, it hurt to hear it.

"No rough spots?" she continued.

"A few little arguments here and there, of course," Sean said. "That's normal, isn't it? It's natural. Nothing much, though, at all."

Olivia looked around at the beautiful home. Obviously Sean did his best to keep Raine happy. It seemed like he gave her whatever she wanted. Many women would die for a life like this.

"Tell me again about the weekend." Olivia felt the need for more details now. "When did Raine leave exactly, when was she supposed to return?"

"She left by herself and planned to fly back alone," Sean repeated. "It was a bachelorette party for one of her good friends, Sloane, who's finally tying the knot. Sloane's a fine woman, very fine."

"Glad to hear that," said Olivia.

"The girls decided to go down to Key West for the celebration," Sean continued. "There's lots to do there, great food, music, beaches."

Olivia knew that only too well. It was also a romantic spot to celebrate in.

"There's even a gallery down there where Raine sometimes sells her photographs," Sean continued. "So, Raine wanted to get down there a bit early, give herself a little extra time. I expected her home right after the party, like the rest of her friends."

"Did anyone know she was staying down there longer?" Olivia asked.

"Not that I know of." Sean was quick on the draw. "Raine likes to take her camera and explore all kinds of neighborhoods and winding trails," Sean went on. "It's her form of relaxation."

"I remember that well," said Olivia.

Sean turned and looked at her intensely. "I'm glad you do," he replied. "After the baby was born it seems Raine needed more and more relaxation."

"A child can be demanding," Olivia replied.

"I guess she can be," Sean halfheartedly agreed.

"Is there any other reason Raine wanted to stay down there longer?" Olivia asked.

"None that I know." Sean got nervous. "Why would there be?"

"I have no idea," said Olivia, "none at all. But I have to find out."

Sean's voice suddenly got louder. "I know you can find her and when you do, please tell her I'm not happy about this! At all! Clea needs her! And her mother needs to go home. Tell Raine to remember that."

"I will," said Olivia, startled by his outburst. "But how do I find her? What's the next step?"

"You find out for yourself. You have great instincts, I immediately felt it," Sean replied.

Olivia was pleased by the comment. She also felt eager to jump into the case, to find her old friend and say hello again after all these years.

"Okay, so who should I talk to first?" Olivia asked.

"Speak to Pietra," Sean responded instantly. "Pietra lives in Miami and runs a smart little boutique in the middle of town. She organized the bachelorette party, knows everyone who attended, exactly what happened, and probably also knows where Raine is hiding out."

"Hiding out?" Olivia was startled. "You believe she's hiding from something?"

"I don't mean it like that." Sean's eyes suddenly narrowed. "I mean she's not here, is she? No one knows where she is. To me, that's hiding!"

CHAPTER FOUR

Sean rented Olivia a car and she drove straight to Pietra's boutique in the heart of Miami. Sean told Olivia he'd been in touch with Pietra, who was now eagerly expecting her. Hardly knowing what to think, Olivia quickly drove out of the suburb and through the center of the city to Little Havana. The lively Cuban influence was reflected in the cafes and cigar shops that lined the colorful streets. Right in the middle of it all stood Pietra's snazzy boutique, with large glass windows and loud, ringing chimes on the door.

Olivia parked across the street, got out of the car and straightened her skirt, and shook her long hair back over her shoulders. The day was growing warmer and humid and Olivia was hot and thirsty. As she crossed the street and entered the colorful, trendy boutique the lively chimes rang out, announcing her arrival.

Before Olivia knew it, Pietra, a striking young Latino woman with dark, curly hair, a flashing smile, and dressed in an orange print dress, came running up to Olivia.

"You must be Olivia, you're beautiful." Her words couldn't get out fast enough. "It's sooo sweet of you to come down here and give us a hand."

Olivia warmed to Pietra immediately, delighted by her wide open manner.

"Come to the back room with me. We can talk privately," Pietra bubbled on, taking Olivia's hand and half pulling her through the sparkly store, filled with wonderful dresses, jewelry, handbags, and gifts of all kinds.

"You have a wonderful shop," Olivia murmured as she followed her.

"I know, I know," said Pietra. "Everybody comes here and loves it. Then they come back again. There's something here for everyone."

Despite herself, Olivia smiled. Pietra had a childlike, bubbly enthusiasm about her that was contagious. It made sense that Raine would have a friend like this.

"You and Raine are best friends?" Olivia asked as Pietra whisked her into the back room, closed the door, and pulled out a plush, embroidered chair for Olivia to sit on.

"Sit down here, darling," she said. "It's sooo comfortable." Then Pietra plopped herself down right beside Olivia. "Of course we're best friends," she went on then. "All our friends are best friends. Do you want a cup of tea?"

"No, just some water, thanks," Olivia answered, struck with a moment of sadness, wishing she could be part of these best friends as well.

Pietra jumped up to bring Olivia water. Not only was it startling to be here, it was wonderful, like a vacation from her life. Olivia pulled herself up quickly then. She had to remember why she was here in the first place. Something out of the ordinary had happened. Raine could be in danger. Olivia was here to help.

"Are you worried about Raine?" Olivia immediately asked Pietra, as she returned with a tall, blue glass of water.

"Of course I'm worried, very much worried." Pietra popped back down on the little chair she'd placed beside Olivia. "We are all terribly worried. In fact, Nessa called me crying last night."

That surprised Olivia. It wasn't the impression she'd had from Sean. He'd told her the girls all thought that Raine would be back shortly.

"Sean said you all thought it was nothing, that Raine would be back in a little while," Olivia responded.

Pietra stopped and looked directly at Olivia. "That was yesterday," she said. "Or the day before? I can't remember. Of course in the beginning we all just laughed. Now no one is laughing. Not any of us."

Olivia sat up straighter. "Why hasn't someone contacted the police?"

"Sean won't let us." Pietra zoned in as well. "He refuses to believe Raine is really missing. And he's afraid what everyone will think or do, if it becomes public. Actually, I was the one who convinced him to call you."

"Really?" Olivia was startled.

"Yes, I read all about what happened to you in Key West and how you were brave and found the killer."

Olivia's heart began beating harder. "Thank you," she replied.

"You're amazing," Pietra went on. "All the girls thought so, including Raine."

That meant a great deal to Olivia. She'd had no idea Raine cared anything about her anymore.

"I knew we needed help with this, and I told Sean that," Pietra continued. "I said if you're not going to call the police right away and tell them, at least call Raine's best friend from college down. She's smart. She'll help us."

Olivia felt out of her depth. "But you need a real detective," she said. "There's protocol when people go missing."

"I don't believe in protocols and you're better than most real detectives." Pietra leaned closer to her. "And you know Raine. You'll care more about her. It matters to you to bring her home."

That was true for certain; Olivia did care. Having seen Sean and now being with Pietra, Olivia felt close to Raine once again. There was no choice but to dive in fully.

"Okay, tell me what you think is going on," Olivia asked Pietra. "Fill me in on everything."

"Sweetheart, by now I am convinced something is definitely wrong." Pietra's voice got lower as she leaned closer. "Raine is definitely missing. It's obvious, isn't it?"

"Obvious to who? All her friends?" asked Olivia.

"I think so," said Pietra. "Why wouldn't she be back by now? Raine's a smart girl. She knows her way around. She even goes down to Key West often. There's a gallery there that sells her photos. They're beautiful, you know."

"That's what I heard," said Olivia. "So she's familiar with the place, comfortable there?"

"Absolutely," said Pietra. "Something had to have happened." Pietra started wringing her hands.

"Like what?" Olivia suddenly felt chilled. "Was Raine depressed or upset? Could she have decided to run away from it all?"

"That's ridiculous." Pietra flushed. "Of course we all get upset here and there, but what would she be running away from? You saw her house! You saw her husband. Did you meet Clea yet?"

"Not yet," said Olivia.

"Raine has it all." Pietra's voice grew husky. "And she realizes it. Her husband dotes on her, so does everyone. He's the kind of husband everyone dreams of. There's nothing she has to run away from."

Pietra jumped up, ran to a nearby counter, and poured herself a cup of tea.

Olivia got up and ran over to her. "Tell me about the bachelorette party," she asked quickly. "What happened at it?"

"Just the usual." Pietra shrugged her shoulders. "We were all dancing and drinking and had a little fun."

"Dancing with who?" asked Olivia.

"Whoever was there. We were in the Sancho Hotel. It's well known, fun, crowded, everyone joins in. They have lots of bachelorette parties." Pietra drank all her tea in one gulp.

"Everyone at the party had a good time?" asked Olivia.

"Of course they did, why wouldn't they?" Pietra replied. "We're all so happy for Sloane. After plenty of rough times with miserable guys, she's finally getting married."

"Tell me about Sloane," Olivia quickly jumped in. She realized that she had to know everything about everyone who attended, fast.

"There's nothing to tell. She's our age, beautiful, works here in town," Pietra started. "Sloane had plenty of guys that weren't good for her and then she finally met Lance. They went out for a long time and he wanted her badly. Finally, he convinced her to walk down the aisle. What's the big deal? We made her a bachelorette party to celebrate."

"I need details, Pietra." Olivia zeroed in. "Who was at the party? What happened?"

"It was fine, believe me, I've been to tons of these things. Nothing out of the ordinary," Pietra repeated, pouring herself another cup of tea.

"Are Raine and Sloane close?" Olivia felt as if she were cornering Pietra now.

"Of course they are, very close," said Pietra. "In fact, Sean and Raine contribute to the charity Sloane works at. We are all good people, every one of us, and, more important, good friends."

"I know you are." Olivia put her hand on Pietra's arm to calm her. "But something has gone wrong. I have to ask you all these questions."

Pietra took a long breath. "I know you do, honey, but you can't begin to suspect any one of us, ever! That's completely crazy. Promise me."

"I don't suspect anyone yet," Olivia answered.

"Yet?" Pietra's eyes opened wide, alarmed.

"I'll have to suspect something eventually, won't I?" Olivia answered. "That's my job, isn't it? It's possible someone could have done something to Raine."

"Nobody we know did anything to her!" Pietra was emphatic. "They never would! It's out of the question!"

"Could she have been taken?" Olivia asked somberly then.

"Taken? Kidnapped? Absolutely not! How could it be?" Pietra was shaken to the core by the thought of it. "What would they take her for?"

"Money. Ransom." Olivia looked at Pietra closely. "Raine's obviously got lots of money and there are plenty of drug gangs in these parts."

"No, that didn't happen to her!" Pietra insisted, agitated.

19

"Or maybe someone has something against her husband, Sean?" Olivia wasn't letting up.

"Crazy, that's crazy," Pietra insisted. "Sean's a wonderful man, helps everyone. There's nothing in the world to have against him." Pietra shuddered.

Pietra was unwilling to consider any option. She was probably holding something back, thought Olivia.

"You have to tell me everything you know, Pietra." Olivia grew firmer. "Otherwise, you're obstructing justice."

"Now you're accusing *me*?" Pietra was totally horrified.

"No, I'm not, not at all," Olivia jumped in. "I'm just letting you know how important it is to tell me every single thing you might know."

"Okay, listen to me, I'll tell you something." Pietra trembled and tried her best to comply. "But you have to swear you won't say a word to anyone."

"I don't know if I can swear to that," said Olivia.

"You have to." Pietra stamped her foot hard.

"Don't put me into a box." Olivia became adamant. "We're looking for Raine, something could have happened to her. I need to be able to use all the information I get."

"But you can't say a word to Sean, ever!" Pietra's eyes flashed.

"What do you have to tell me? Say it, please!" Olivia felt fire rising in her as well.

"Raine was really drunk at the party," Pietra went on in a hushed tone. "I even told her to lay off the booze a little, but she just laughed at me."

That was like Raine, Olivia recalled, to drink a lot at parties. "Has she become an alcoholic?" Olivia asked alarmed.

"No, not at all," Pietra said firmly, "but that night she was drinking really heavily. We were all having fun, it was a good time. There were even a few strippers dancing for us."

"And?"

"One of them kept dancing too close to Raine." Pietra's eyes rolled. "We all noticed it. At least I did. He was really cute, too! Too cute for his own good. But I can't be sure of exactly what happened between them. I was drinking heavily too."

"You weren't too drunk to notice that he was cute, though," Olivia zeroed in.

Pietra began laughing now.

Olivia was appalled. "What happened with Raine and the stripper?"

Pietra stopped laughing on a dime. "You just said it, not me. I swore not to say a word about it to anyone."

"A word about what?" Olivia stood tall, confronting her.

"About Raine and the stripper. Okay, it's not such a big tragedy. I think Raine *may* have played around with this stripper, cheated on Sean. These things happen. It's just the heat of the moment. It happens and then it's over with fast."

Olivia felt both saddened and sickened. "Maybe this time it didn't end so fast?"

Pietra paled. "Why the hell not?"

"Could be Raine's still with him?" Olivia said.

"That's completely ridiculous." Pietra was adamant. "It was a one-night stand. They happen all the time."

"Could be the stripper had an accomplice who nabbed her?" Olivia was purposely turning up the heat. She wanted to hear all Pietra had to say.

"It's crazy! You're crazy!" Pietra spun around. "Gals sleep with these guys all the time. It's just for the moment and then it's over. It means nothing to anyone!"

Olivia grew chilled and silent.

"What's the matter with you?" Pietra flared up. "Who are you anyway? You think you're too good for us?"

"Not at all," said Olivia slowly. "It's just that playing around does mean something. It means something to a lot of people now, doesn't it? Raine's gone, isn't she? She hasn't returned."

"So go to the hotel in Key West and see what you can find there!" Pietra shot back. "Drive or take a small plane. It will only take a little while."

"I will," Olivia quickly agreed. "Tell me who this stripper is. Give me all his contact information. I'm going to meet him myself."

CHAPTER FIVE

Olivia drove down to Key West along the narrow, scenic highway bordering the ocean. As she rolled down the car window the warm ocean breezes drifted in, soothing her. It was wonderful to be near the water again. It was healing and also strange to be headed back down to Key West so soon. Olivia couldn't help but feel that it was almost as if she were being called back, had left too soon. As if there was definitely unfinished business for her to complete.

As she approached her destination, a flood of memories washed over her. Olivia recalled the magical night she and Todd had become engaged, with his vows of undying love. Olivia had felt transported to a place of such beauty, safety, and love. It seemed as if her entire world had turned a corner, with everything finally falling into its rightful place. Somehow at that moment, all the pain and disappointment she'd gone through in her life before made perfect sense. Her love for Todd had washed it all away.

Later, as the investigation into his shocking death went forward, when Olivia learned that Todd had still been deeply involved with an ex-girlfriend, her whole world cracked into pieces. The joy of their relationship turned into ashes. Now, as she drove down the familiar streets, Olivia realized that both the bitterness she felt for Todd and the love still lingered.

It wasn't so easy to erase the wonderful times they had shared throughout the five intense months of their relationship. The connection between them had been perfect right from the start. It was wonderful being able to share everything so deeply with another person. Olivia had never experienced that before. Being with Todd had opened up parts of her that could be spontaneous, adventurous, daring even. Her relationship with Paul had been different. He'd always been good to her, dependable, romantic even. Yet there had been a gulf between them that could not be breached, an undercurrent of loneliness.

But this trip to Key West wasn't about her and Todd. Olivia's thoughts quickly turned to Raine. Was she still down in Key West, extending her vacation? It was possible, but didn't seem likely. Why wouldn't she be in touch with anyone? Olivia had to talk to everyone who knew Raine down here, trace whatever footprints she could find. She also had to be absolutely positive that Raine and the stripper had actually been together. Sean had said their marriage was terrific. Friends often imagined all kinds of things about each

22

other, especially when they were drinking at bachelorette parties. If what Pietra said was true, though, it would tell Olivia a lot. Not only about Raine's marriage and what was going on in her life, but where she might be hiding right now.

Olivia looked at the time as she drove. The trip was going quickly. As soon as she arrived in Key West her plan was to check into her hotel and then go straight to the Sancho. Pietra had called and found out that the stripper, Luigi, was scheduled to be dancing there tonight. Pietra also made a reservation for Olivia at a hotel a few blocks away from the one she and Todd had stayed at. Olivia didn't want to return to her old hotel or remain at the Sancho for too long.

Before she knew it, Olivia turned off the highway at the familiar exit for Key West. It would be only a few moments before she was back in town again. Tears stung her eyes as she passed through the familiar streets and promenade. How was it possible that she was returning here alone?

*

By the time Olivia checked into her hotel, changed, and then arrived at the Sancho it was early evening, with the light starting to dim. To her surprise, the Sancho was imposing, set back from the street, with a long, rolling lawn in front. Olivia had expected something different, a place that was a bit sleazy or sordid, but the Sancho seemed to be mainstream, hosting parties and events of all kinds. A cobbled walkway led up through the lawn to the main entrance.

Olivia drove around to the back parking lot. She parked, got out, and walked slowly to the front and then into the lobby. The place was hopping, filled with cheerful visitors thoroughly enjoying their stay.

Olivia went straight to the front desk and asked a very slim woman who sat behind it whether Luigi was there yet.

The woman cast a nervous glance at Olivia. "Yes, he's here," she replied in a flippant tone. "Why?"

"Great, where can I find him?" Olivia continued, bypassing the second part of her comment.

"Luigi's in the club in the back, the Requiem, where he always is," the woman replied. "In fact, a bachelorette party's starting there in about half an hour. Are you going to it?"

"Not that I know of." Olivia tried to smile, but the woman frowned. "Well, thanks anyway," said Olivia as she turned and made her way to the club at the back.

Olivia walked through one hallway after another and finally at the very end, double doors with a sign "The Requiem" over them greeted her. This had to be the place she was looking for. Grinding music was playing loudly inside, and flashing lights were blinking over the sign. Raine had been here just a few nights ago, Olivia realized. The thought of it was mind-boggling.

Olivia pushed the doors open, almost hoping to see Raine waiting there for her. Instead, the place was dark, musty, and mostly empty, filled with tables and a long bar. Olivia stood there looking around for any sign of life, someone she could talk to.

"Can I help you?" a man's voice called out from behind her. "The party doesn't start for about half an hour yet."

Olivia spun around. A man in his late forties, dressed in dark slacks and an open shirt, stood there with a notebook in his hand. It seemed as though he were in charge of everything.

"I've come to talk to Luigi." Olivia was suddenly uneasy.

The man stopped and looked at Olivia oddly. "Luigi's dancing later tonight. Is he a friend of yours?"

"No, not exactly." Olivia took a few steps away. "He's a friend of a friend."

"He'll be out later," the man replied. "There's a party here tonight, are you a guest?"

"No, I'm not," said Olivia plainly. "My friend was a guest at another bachelorette party that Luigi danced at."

The man, puzzled, scrutinized Olivia more carefully now. "And what about your friend?" he asked, trying to understand what was up.

Olivia didn't know if she should tell him that her friend had gone missing, never returned home. Should she tell him that it was an urgent matter, that Olivia was here to find her? The information had not yet been made public. The man would ask why the police hadn't been called in. And it would be a good question.

"I just need to talk to Luigi for a few minutes," Olivia said instead. "It won't take long. It's an important matter."

To Olivia's surprise, the man nodded his head. "Yeah, all kinds of people want to talk to Luigi. Okay, come with me," he said quickly. "Just a few minutes, though. You wait over here near the bar and I'll tell Luigi you're here. What's your name anyway? You look familiar."

"Olivia Wells," Olivia answered, suddenly realizing that this man may have seen her on the news when she was searching for Todd's killer.

The man became more interested now. "Your name's familiar too. Will your name be familiar to Luigi?"

"I doubt it," said Olivia. "I'm here to talk to him about Raine Merkin."

"I get it. Okay." The man backed off. "I'll bring Luigi to you right now."

*

In a few minutes, Luigi came out the back door. Tall and swarthy, he was dressed in a rough, sleeveless shirt, with dark hair falling over his forehead. A large tattoo was plastered all over his forearm.

"What's going on?" Luigi asked, eyeing Olivia closely.

"Thanks for coming to talk to me," Olivia replied, trying to buy some space and time.

"What's going on? I'm a busy man," Luigi repeated, rubbing his sweaty face.

"Do you remember a woman named Raine Merkin?" Olivia had no choice but to jump right in.

Luigi smirked. "Honey, if I remembered all of the ladies who come to this place, I'd be some kind of genius. And I'm not."

Despite herself, Olivia smiled. Luigi may not have been a genius, but he was certainly engaging.

"Raine was at a bachelorette party here just a few days ago," Olivia filled him in.

"Yeah, and?" None of it was computing.

"Raine's tall, beautiful, with long brown hair and big green eyes." Olivia tried to jog his memory. "I heard she enjoyed your dancing a lot."

"They all enjoy my dancing." Luigi grinned suddenly. "Oh yeah, the green eyes I remember. Not too many with green eyes like that. She's one hell of a bombshell, isn't she? And that lady certainly knows what she wants."

Olivia was startled. "What does she want?"

"What does everyone want when they come to a party? Fun, excitement, pleasure! Nothing wrong with that, is there?"

Olivia was caught short.

"What's up now? What do you want to talk to me for?" Luigi was getting restless.

"Did you two sleep together?" Olivia pulled out all the stops.

"Whoa, what kind of question is that? Who are you, anyway, some kind of a nut?" Luigi was taken aback. "You think I'm going to tell you that? Hell, I don't even know you. If I told tales out of school, you know what would happen to my reputation?"

"This is important, Luigi, I need to know," Olivia spoke over him.

"Why? Who are you anyhow?" he balked.

"Raine never came home from the bachelorette party," Olivia stated intensely. "I'm a close friend of hers. We're all looking for her now."

"Wait a minute, back up!" Luigi rubbed his face with the red handkerchief scarf that was tied around his neck. "What do you mean she never came home?"

"There's a search going on," Olivia repeated.

"Who's searching? The cops and everything?" He seemed to be growing nervous.

"Not the cops yet. Just family and friends for now."

"Listen, you get the cops on this immediately." He seemed upset. "They know what to do when this stuff happens. It's nothing to play around with."

"We're not playing," Olivia defended herself.

"Sure you're playing," Luigi answered. "There are all kinds of freaks down here in Key West. Anything could have happened. Why the hell are you asking me?"

"One of Raine's friends said that you and she got it together at the party," Olivia said.

"So we fooled around a little, so the hell what? It happens all the time. Doesn't mean I saw her after that."

"You had no contact at all with her later?" Olivia needed to be positive.

"Nothing, none at all," Luigi insisted. "What happens at the Sancho stays at the Sancho. I'm not exactly looking for a long-term relationship with these broads. And neither are they, most of the time."

"Most of the time? Was Raine? Did she want more from you?" Olivia couldn't let it go. "Did she ask to see you again?"

"Absolutely not," Luigi retorted. "There wasn't even a hint of it." He looked so astonished at the suggestion that Olivia believed him on the spot.

"Okay, okay," Olivia said.

"There's nothing okay about it," he retorted. "Listen, you go check out those dames who were at the party with her. Someone knows where she is right now. Don't let them fool you. They talk to each other about everything."

"Maybe," Olivia replied.

"No maybes about it, honey." Luigi swooped over closer to Olivia then. "It's definite. Now I'm even remembering there was one dame who kept shadowing Raine wherever she went that night. We needed time together alone and couldn't get rid of her. It's coming back to me, her name was Nessa. She had to see every little thing Raine was doing. Finally, we lost her. But it took some time."

Olivia would have to talk to all the women carefully, especially Nessa. But she was also fascinated to realize that it seemed Pietra had been right. It was clear that Raine and Luigi had hooked up. Was Raine just looking for thrills for the night or was there something much darker going on in her life? Right now, it was definitely starting to seem like there was trouble way beyond what anyone knew.

*

After leaving the bar, Olivia immediately put a call in to Sean.

"Where are you? What's happening?" He was completely on edge. "Pietra told me you drove back down to Key West."

"Yes, I did," replied Olivia, "and I didn't want to call you until I had something definite to say."

"So what do you have?" Sean's voice grew higher.

"Sit down a minute," Olivia replied.

"I'm standing and it's fine," Sean replied. "Did you find out where she is, what happened to her?"

Olivia couldn't bring herself to tell Sean about Luigi yet, certainly not over the phone.

"Not exactly," said Olivia, "but we've got to bring in the police immediately. Can you fly down to Key West as soon as possible?"

He cleared his throat.

"Why?" he asked.

She took a deep breath.

"I don't think Raine's coming home so fast."

CHAPTER SIX

Before Olivia met up with Sean the next morning, she told him to go straight to the police station. She'd meet him there. Olivia wanted to first go there alone, and see if Wayne or Lorna were there. She wanted to talk to them about Raine before Sean arrived on the scene. Wayne and Lorna had been the primary detectives she'd worked with on Todd's case and were usually there at this hour of the morning.

After a quick breakfast, Olivia drove to the familiar building. She parked outside and walked through the main doors. To her delight, when Olivia walked in, she recognized the officer at the front desk, Gabe.

"Hi, Gabe," said Olivia with a smile.

"Olivia! This is the last thing I expected today," Gabe replied, coming out from behind the desk to greet her.

Olivia felt strangely relieved to be back there. It felt like she'd never left, as though her work with the department was ongoing.

"What brings you back here so soon?" Gabe asked. "I thought you were back home by now, getting settled."

"Lots of reasons," said Olivia. "But I was wondering if Wayne or Lorna happened to be in? I need to talk to them."

"Sure they're here, they're here every day," Gabe answered. "Hold on a minute and I'll tell them you're visiting."

Gabe picked up the phone and Olivia's heart started beating faster. How strange it would be to see both of them so soon. She wondered what they would make of her visit. Olivia certainly never expected to be back here so soon.

To Olivia's delight, before she knew it, Wayne was walking down the hallway intently, coming toward her. Dressed in his usual khaki pants, breezy and handsome with his sandy hair ruffled, he looked puzzled. Olivia was surprised at how good it was to see him.

"Hi, how are you? What are you doing here?" Wayne asked, concerned.

Olivia smiled. "A lot has happened since I've seen you."

"What's wrong?" Wayne became flustered.

Olivia breathed deeply, happy for the opportunity to talk to him again. "There's trouble again," she murmured.

"With who? Todd's family? Are they bothering you?" Wayne looked upset. "I've heard through the grapevine that they're not adjusting to Todd's death at all."

"No, it has nothing to do with Todd at all," Olivia answered as they both paused for a moment. It was a brand new playing field and she had to get used to it. Olivia was here in a completely different capacity now.

"Who's the trouble with?" Wayne looked perturbed.

"Can we go and talk in your office?" asked Olivia.

"Sure," said Wayne as they both quickly turned and walked down the hallway into the office Wayne shared with Lorna.

"Lorna will be back in a minute, what's going on?" Wayne asked again. "We all thought you were doing fine back up in New York."

"I thought so too," said Olivia as Wayne sat behind his desk and she took a chair opposite him. "I actually did return to work for a little while."

"And?" Wayne asked, as the door opened and Lorna, dressed in her usual pants and crisp shirt, walked in.

"Olivia?" Lorna exclaimed, looking confused.

"She just arrived," Wayne reported. "I haven't heard what's going on yet. Sit down."

Lorna threw Wayne an odd glance, grabbed a wooden chair, and plopped herself down on it.

"Okay, let's have it," she said to Olivia. "What's wrong now?"

Olivia shivered a moment. Lorna seemed tougher and more abrasive than she'd remembered. Lorna seemed irritated to see Olivia now, as well.

"I received a call from a friend's husband when I was in New York," Olivia started. "My friend's name is Raine Merkin, and she lives in Miami."

Wayne nodded, as if to say, I'm listening, go ahead! Lorna showed no reaction.

"Raine went to a routine bachelorette party in Key West a few days ago," Olivia proceeded. "She never returned home."

"Wait a minute, what are you saying exactly?" Wayne looked perturbed.

"Repeat that," Lorna echoed.

"Raine's husband, Sean, called and asked me to come down to Florida to help him find out where she is," Olivia repeated slowly. "He's worried something may have happened to her."

"That's a tall order," Wayne breathed.

"Why did he call you and not us?" Lorna wasn't going along with it.

"He heard about the work I did finding Todd's killer," said Olivia, hoping Lorna would not be offended.

29

"You mean he heard that it was because of you that Todd's case busted wide open," Wayne said, getting up from behind the desk.

"Something like that," said Olivia.

"Okay, so he heard it," Lorna conceded. "How long has Raine been gone?"

"About three or four days," Olivia realized.

"Why hasn't he come here and talked to us by now?" Lorna asked immediately and Wayne nodding, seeming to agree.

"Sean hasn't been sure Raine's missing," said Olivia. "He didn't want to create a public stir, or unwanted publicity. Actually, he keeps thinking Raine will return any second."

"But she hasn't, has she?" Lorna stood up now, too.

"That's not unusual," Wayne intercepted. "Many family members think that."

"Who is this guy anyway?" Lorna paid no attention to Wayne, cut him off.

"You'll actually meet him yourself in a few minutes," said Olivia then. "Sean's on his way down to the police station right now as we speak."

"He sent you ahead of him to tell us about this?" Wayne was displeased.

"Not exactly." Olivia was beginning to feel flustered. "Sean first asked me to talk to Raine's friends at the party to see if anyone knew where she was."

"That's our job." Lorna was disgruntled. "First you go to law enforcement."

"Did you talk to her friends yet?" Wayne interrupted in a calmer tone.

"I started to." Olivia felt reassured by Wayne's presence. "I talked to one friend, Pietra, who told me to come down to the Sancho, where the party was held."

"That's a well-known place for bachelorette parties," Wayne murmured.

"And did you go to the Sancho?" Lorna was grilling Olivia now.

"Yes, I did. In fact, I spoke to someone there," Olivia answered matter-of-factly, not wanting to get into the whole story yet.

"Did you tell Sean what you found out so far?" Wayne sensed Olivia's hesitation.

"I told him I definitely thought something was wrong and that we should go to the police immediately," Olivia replied.

"What made you think that?" Lorna was all over it.

"Raine's been gone too long," Olivia replied, vaguely. She had no intention of going into details with Lorna.

"But what exactly did you find at the Sancho that made you think something was wrong?" Lorna examined Olivia closely.

"That place looks good on the outside, but is grubby as hell," Wayne said under his breath.

"Time is of the essence when someone goes missing," Lorna repeated. "Everyone knows that."

"Sean hasn't been able to face the fact that Raine's actually missing," Olivia repeated curtly.

"Tell us more about Sean." Wayne was fully engaged.

"He's an established business owner in Miami," Olivia replied. "Sean's well known; a good man, pillar of the community, involved with charities, the church, the works."

"That doesn't necessarily impress me," Lorna quipped. "The best can become the worst. We'll have to question him thoroughly."

"Stop it!" Wayne wouldn't allow Lorna to go on. "There's no reason to point a finger at a guy who has to be in a lot of pain."

"I'm not pointing a finger," Lorna snapped. "He's the next of kin."

"You'll meet Sean yourself in a few minutes." Olivia felt the need to calm both of them down.

"Lorna's upset that Sean didn't come here first," said Wayne. "But many people don't, for exactly the reason you mentioned. They can't believe it's really happening. They're convinced a friend knows something. Or they expect their loved one to just walk in the door."

At that very moment there was a knock on the door. Lorna went over briskly and pulled it open. Gabe stood there beside Sean.

"He says you're expecting him." Gabe pointed to Sean, who stood there looking dazed.

"We are expecting him," Wayne replied, waving Sean into the room as Gabe backed away.

Wayne walked over to Sean briskly. "Good to meet you," he said. "So sorry for the difficulty you're in."

"Thank you," said Sean, nervous and pale, as if this were the last place in the world he wanted to be. "I just flew down here this morning. What happens now?"

CHAPTER SEVEN

What happens now is anyone's guess, thought Olivia, terrified at the prospect of watching Sean's life fall apart.

"Olivia's filled us in on the basics." Wayne spoke to Sean directly. "Of course we need to know a lot more. Next step, we officially open a case."

Sean looked around the room, as if he were searching for a way out of the nightmare he'd been thrust into.

"Please sit down," Wayne went on.

Sean sat down and for a moment looked as if he were about to bolt. His anxiety was definitely increasing.

"Raine still hasn't returned," Sean finally said, mournfully.

"I need the dates of the party, when she left for it, how long she's been gone." Wayne took it from there.

"I have it all written down," Sean replied, pulling a piece of paper out of his pocket.

Wayne took the paper and looked over it carefully. "I also need your wife's photo. As soon as the case is open, we'll put her photo up on our website and check with other vicinities to see if she's been spotted. We also check hospitals."

Sean cringed. "Raine's not in a hospital," he gasped. "I'm sure of that."

"We'll do as much as we can," Wayne continued frankly. "We're set up to handle all kinds of emergency situations, including kidnapping. What we do not do, however, is actively search for a person who does not want to be found."

"Raine wants to be found, I'm certain of it!" Sean's eye began twitching. "Why would you even suggest she doesn't?"

"Wayne's saying that in many cases, people leave intentionally," Lorna jumped in. "They run away, start a new life."

"Raine did not leave intentionally!" Sean looked insulted. "I can guarantee that."

"Really? How?" asked Lorna.

Wayne paid no attention to Lorna's comment, just continued instructing Sean on protocol.

"When a missing person's case is reported, the first question is how long have they been missing? If you say anything less than twenty-four hours you will be instructed to go home and wait until twenty-four hours have passed. Then we file a report."

"It's been much longer than that," Sean tried to interrupt.

"Additionally," Wayne continued, "in order for the police to launch a missing person investigation, we have to know the person did not leave home of their own free will. If a person is missing because they wanted to leave, there will be no report or investigation in most jurisdictions."

"I guarantee she didn't leave of her own accord. Raine had a great life. She was happy." Sean's voice grew louder. "And it's been longer than twenty-four hours!"

"Yes, it has, I see that," Wayne replied.

"A lot can happen in twenty-four hours when a person is missing," Lorna broke in. "Just because the police may not think the person is in danger, this does not mean it is true."

"Are you telling me that Raine is in danger?" Sean began twisting in his chair.

"She certainly could be," breathed Lorna. "You have to be ready for that."

"But I'm not," Sean growled at her.

"This is a complicated situation we are embarking upon." Wayne tried to tone it down. "You need to know the facts and what to expect. After the police file a report, they will then let you know if and when your loved one is found."

"If and when?" Sean breathed hard.

"We do what we can," Lorna piped up. "But most of the time we can't search fully enough for each person who's gone."

"What do you mean you can't search fully enough?" Sean obviously disliked Lorna.

"We do what we can but our resources are limited," Lorna continued. "The demands on our time are enormous. Many missing person's cases are pursued for a while. Then they go cold, leads dry up."

Olivia was disturbed that Lorna was being so pessimistic.

Sean seemed to grow more agitated. "Okay, what now?" he said.

"You have other options as well," Wayne quickly responded. "You can hire your own private investigators. Many do. Private investigators have all kinds of training and tactics to do a complete search. All kinds of leads are dug up and carefully followed. Massive searches are arranged, publicity planned for. They get the case out there."

Sean sighed. "I'm not hiring any private investigators," he grumbled. "There are plenty of people who will help me. I'll handle this on my own."

"For starters, you'll have to make posters and paste them around," Wayne continued. "You'll also have to gather volunteers to give them out and start searching for leads. The more publicity the better, of course."

Sean cringed. "This is going to embarrass everybody," he muttered.

"You're convinced your wife is still alive?" Lorna snapped, turning on him forcefully.

"I am," Sean insisted. "In fact, I'm positive of it."

Olivia took a swift, painful breath. She remembered how harsh Lorna could be, pushing people to their limits to rattle them and get them to slip up.

"Raine wasn't depressed, impulsive, or tired of the marriage?" Lorna was going in for the kill. "She wasn't eager to get away forever?"

Sean looked both stunned and offended. "Raine and I have a wonderful relationship," he insisted. "We're happy together and always will be."

"There are plenty of people who will testify to that?" Lorna wanted to be sure.

"Yes, there are," Sean insisted.

"Where do you think Raine is, Sean?" Wayne asked in a more soothing tone.

"I have no idea," Sean was swift to reply. "But we've barely touched the iceberg. Olivia hasn't had a chance yet to talk to all Raine's friends."

"When did it become Olivia's job to talk to Raine's friends?" Lorna jumped on his comment. "This is a job for professionals."

"Olivia will do just fine." Sean became irritated. "In fact, Olivia and Raine were close friends in college."

"That doesn't qualify Olivia to be a detective," Lorna insisted.

Wayne threw Lorna a strange glance. "Olivia did wonderfully in helping us find Todd's killer," he remarked. "I can see why Sean would turn to her now."

Lorna turned away from Wayne, disgruntled. "Whether or not Sean hires an investigator, he has to give us detailed information now," Lorna proceeded. "We'll need your wife's photo, her age, her occupation. You said she was down here for a bachelorette party? Did she come down to Key West for any other reason?"

"Raine is thirty-four, a wife and mother," Sean began to reply. "She's a freelance photographer and yes, she comes down to Key West from time to time. Some of her photos sell in a gallery here."

Lorna and Wayne seemed interested in that piece of information. "Give us the name of the gallery owner and we'll talk to them," said Wayne. "He can give us a better idea of who knew her."

"Raine's a very private person," Sean exclaimed.

"Not anymore," said Lorna. "Every little thing about her life is going to be scrutinized now. Anything can be a clue to find her. We'll need to know the places she usually went to in Miami as well. Who were the people she was in touch with on a daily basis? You're sure you know everything about her?"

"Of course I do," Sean answered tartly. "We're incredibly close, discuss every little thing that's going on."

"This has to be very nerve-wracking for you," Wayne added.

"You can say that again," Sean agreed. "And I was hoping to keep it quiet."

Lorna scoffed. "If you're lucky we can get this all over the news. You've got to get as many people searching for her as possible." Lorna shot Olivia a troubled glance. "Why didn't you tell him to get here sooner?"

"I suggested it." Olivia felt under the gun. "As I said, Sean wasn't ready."

"Ready or not, lost time is lost time," Lorna shot back. "You should have told us about it yourself."

"Olivia did just fine," Wayne interrupted, throwing Olivia an encouraging glance. "It's even good of her to be back here now helping after all that she's just gone through."

"Yes, it is good of her." Sean turned and looked at Olivia gratefully.

"It's fine, truly," said Olivia. "There's actually no place I'd rather be."

*

Olivia sat quietly as Wayne and Lorna officially opened the case, made calls, asked Sean routine questions. How long had he known her? Who were the people she saw daily? Were there hobbies or activities she had that he may have known nothing about? Did she show any signs of being suicidal? Leave any notes?

Sean answered each question directly, staring at the floor as he spoke.

"We'll open a tip line immediately," Wayne said as they were finishing up. "Someone could have sighted her, or have some kind of lead. We also need a separate ransom line, in case she's been taken and they want money."

Sean swallowed hard, looked momentarily exhausted.

"Okay, that's it," said Wayne then. "Whether or not you hire an investigator, Sean, is up to you, of course. And Olivia, thanks so much again for your help. You're no longer needed now. You can go back home again and try to unwind."

"Wait a minute, not so fast," Sean objected.

Olivia was glad Sean said something. She felt as if she'd been suddenly tossed to the curb. She didn't want to go home. In fact, she had no intention of doing so. Raine's situation gripped her. There was a lot she could do here and she knew it. At the very least, she could talk to Raine's friends, help organize a search, and monitor the results carefully.

"Olivia's not going anywhere," Sean continued. "I want her staying down here on the case as a private investigator."

Lorna gave both him and Olivia a disturbed glance. "Olivia doesn't have the training," Lorna quipped. "This is an emotional time for you. I'd think it over carefully."

To Olivia's surprise, Sean took Lorna on. "In my book Olivia has all that she needs to do a terrific job," he objected. "I'm hiring Olivia as my private detective right now. There's no law against that, is there?"

Lorna grimaced. "No, there isn't."

"Now, I'd like to go to the bathroom for a minute, if you're done," Sean added.

"Sure, go ahead," Wayne answered.

"I have to go down the hall to speak to the captain, too," Lorna said, as she and Sean got up at the same moment and walked, shoulder to shoulder, out of the room.

The second they left, Wayne closed his eyes. Olivia could see things had gotten rougher between him and Lorna.

"Well, thanks very much for all your help," Wayne said, in a few minutes. "Don't worry, either. I'll stay all over the case. Whether or not Sean hires an investigator, I'll do my best for you guys. You can't have something like this on your shoulders, Olivia. It's time for you to start your new life, isn't it?"

Olivia didn't really know what her new life was supposed to look like. She actually felt more alive down here, working on the case, than she felt back up in New York after she'd returned.

"There's something else I have to tell you," Olivia replied then, almost in a whisper, leaning closer to Wayne. "I didn't want to say it when Sean was here."

"What is it?" Wayne looked interested.

"I spoke to one of the dancers at the bachelorette party," Olivia continued. "His name is Luigi, and he was a stripper there. Raine's friend Pietra said that he and Raine got pretty cozy that night. I wanted to find out more."

Wayne made an odd face. "You asked Luigi if he and Raine got together?"

"Yes, I did," said Olivia. "And he admitted that they fooled around. Luigi also said Raine had a friend at the party, Nessa, who kept following her around, watching every little thing she did."

Wayne shook his head. "I should know all that, and thanks for telling me," he replied. "Seems like sleeping with strippers is routine these days. Raine was probably drunk or high. Or both. Who knows? People do all kinds of things under the influence."

"Doesn't it mean Luigi knows where Raine might be?" Olivia was surprised that Wayne was so nonchalant about it.

"Not necessarily," said Wayne. "These guys fool around with tons of girls, seems to go with the job. There's a party or two there every weekend. The real question is if your friend was on drugs, were dealers involved?"

"They're a rough bunch," Olivia echoed.

"You can say that again," Wayne agreed. "But if I were you, I wouldn't focus on the dealers now. What I would do is speak to Raine's friend Nessa. Who is she and where does she live?"

"I have no idea," said Olivia.

"Well, find out," said Wayne, "and keep me in the loop closely. This is brand new territory for you and I don't like seeing you putting yourself in danger again. The last thing I want is to hear that something's happened to you, that you've also vanished."

CHAPTER EIGHT

As soon as Olivia and Sean left the police station Olivia immediately asked him where Nessa lived.

"Why Nessa?" asked Sean.

"Her name came up a few times," Olivia remarked circumspectly, not wanting to get into any details yet.

"Well, you're in luck," Sean said, "because Nessa lives right down here in Key West. She's a bit odd, if you asked me, she's runs her own scuba diving school. Raine sees her on a regular basis whenever she comes down."

Olivia thought that was exciting. "What's odd about running a scuba diving school?"

Sean seemed taken aback. "Most people think it's odd for a woman," he commented.

Olivia thought how beautiful it must be to spend time deep inside the ocean regularly. "Give me Nessa's contact information," she replied, "and I'll get in touch with her right away."

"You're good, you're terrific." Sean was pleased. "Nothing fazes you, absolutely nothing! You don't miss a beat. I don't care what those detectives at the station said. I definitely want you on the case. There's no question about it."

"Thanks so much." To Olivia's surprise she was thoroughly delighted by the offer. "Accepted!"

Sean smiled broadly.

"And it's a good idea to also get professional investigators involved," Olivia continued. "I'll work alongside them."

Sean bristled. "No, I'm not up for that," he quickly replied. "In my book you're more than enough."

Olivia understood Sean's reluctance and didn't want to press him further now. He'd taken a big step already today, talking to the police. Besides, Wayne assured her that he'd do all he could to help. Olivia knew that Wayne was good for his word and the thought was comforting to her now.

"Okay, I'll give you her contact information and you go speak to Nessa," Sean said. "Then I'm going back to my hotel room to catch up."

Olivia immediately called Nessa, told her she was coming, and then drove straight to the Key West shore.

*

The drive down was familiar to Olivia and she enjoyed heading straight to the ocean again. The Key West shore was home to boats of all kinds, assorted eateries, and a host of scuba diving schools. Nessa's school was called Sunset Divers. On the phone Nessa told Olivia that not only did she teach scuba diving, but arranged for both day and night dives. As Olivia drove along, she wondered if night dives could be dangerous. Was it possible that Raine had gone on one before she disappeared?

As Olivia approached Nessa's school, she looked out at a row of ramshackle buildings, many with diving equipment strewn around outside. It certainly was a unique business for a woman to run, Olivia thought, but why did that make Nessa odd? What was it about her that Sean recoiled from?

Olivia turned a corner then, quickly pulled up in front of Sunset Divers, and parked the car outside.

The minute Olivia stepped out of her car, Nessa came running out of the building, as if she were running from a fire. Dressed in denim shorts, a sloppy, oversized T-shirt, and wide-open sandals, she had long hair that was tangled and damp.

Nessa quickly gave Olivia a quick bear hug. "Thanks for coming to see me," she breathed. "You can't imagine how badly I need to talk. Where is Raine? Please tell me!"

"That's the question, isn't it?" Olivia responded, hoping the meeting would yield some clues. Even though Nessa was frenetic, she was warm and open. Most likely, she'd tell Olivia all she knew.

"I'm also glad to be here," Olivia reassured her.

"Come on inside." Nessa practically pulled Olivia down a ramp then and into the building.

*

The main room inside Nessa's school looked straight out onto the choppy waves. It was open and surprisingly clean. The diving equipment was neatly stored on white wooden shelves and posters of divers hung on the walls. A few plants stood happily on the window sills.

Nessa reached out for Olivia's hands once again as she pulled her onto a wobbly wicker chair.

"What happened, where is Raine?" Nessa repeated, her face growing flushed.

"Just what I was going to ask you," Olivia replied.

"I'm beside myself, can't sleep since I heard this crazy news," Nessa continued.

"You were very close to Raine?" Olivia jumped back in.

"Not were, am! I am very close to Raine, she's one of my best friends!" Nessa seemed shot by a bolt of electricity. "We have great times together—no holds barred. She's down in the Keys somewhere. I'm positive of it."

"Why are you so positive?" Olivia could barely catch her breath around Nessa.

"Because I've known Raine forever. She loves it down here. It's exciting to her." Nessa was babbling.

"How about up in Miami?" Olivia drew back a moment and quieted down, hoping Nessa would do the same.

Nessa jumped up then and walked to the other end of the room, where a big coffee pot stood filled with black coffee, next to some large orange mugs. Olivia got up as well and followed her there.

"Of course, nothing is absolutely perfect everywhere in anyone's life, is it?" Nessa asked as she poured the fresh coffee into two mugs. "Raine and I were such good friends because both of us get antsy and restless. Maybe even a little unhinged?"

"Unhinged?" That didn't sound good. "What do you mean by restless, exactly?" Olivia backtracked, thinking Nessa had the perfect job for someone who got restless, regularly diving down deep into the ocean and returning again.

"I mean Raine was full of life." Nessa tried to smile, but then stopped it. "She got bored with the same old routine, day after day. I'm like that, too."

"Was Raine just restless or was something wrong? Was she upset?" Olivia asked then, remembering their days in college. Raine always had a lively energy, but often a low period would follow a burst of excitement and fun.

Thankfully, Nessa slowed down a moment and handed a coffee mug to Olivia. "No, you're right," she murmured, "I have to be honest. Raine could get upset and we have to say so. After all, we're facing trouble now."

Olivia took the coffee and drank some of it. It was hot and delicious. "Please tell me more about why Raine was upset," she replied, trying her best to stay calm.

Nessa gulped down most of the mug quickly. "It's definitely true, Raine wasn't as happy as she looked. In fact, I recently told Raine a few times to go talk to someone."

"A therapist?" asked Olivia, surprised.

"A counselor, a psychic, someone," Nessa interrupted. "Raine was high a lot these days, more than usual."

Olivia shivered. "High on what? Pot? Cocaine?"

40

Nessa bypassed the question. "Not exactly sure."

"Raine was a drug addict? Involved with dealers?" Olivia was insistent.

"No, not at all." Nessa calmed Olivia down. "Raine just needed some relief from the pain she was in. More pain that usual these days, I guess."

"What pain? Talk to me, Nessa!" Olivia felt herself growing cold. It sounded as if Raine had been in a state of emergency.

"It started right after Raine had the baby," Nessa quickly complied. "She was a different person after the birth. We were all so excited about the baby, but Raine wasn't."

"What do you mean?" Olivia was horrified.

"Raine got very depressed after the baby was born. She really didn't want to hold her or play with her at all," Nessa continued. "Everyone thought it would pass, but it didn't. Sean had to hire a lot of help to care for the child. Raine even had a hard time staying home for long periods. Always running around, here and there."

"How awful, how sad." Olivia found it hard to believe. The happiest time of a woman's life didn't turn out to be that way for Raine.

"Postpartum depression," Nessa murmured. "It happens to more women than you'd ever imagine."

"Was Raine treated for it?" Olivia was distressed.

"No, she wasn't." Nessa put her coffee mug back down on the table. "In fact, nobody wanted to talk about it or call it what it was. I tried, but people ignored me. Lots of women have this, you know."

Olivia was taken aback by how much Nessa knew about it. "I didn't realize that," she said.

"Yeah, it's a silent thing usually," Nessa went on. "People are usually ashamed. Some end up at my scuba diving school. Not too many, but some."

Olivia was aghast, suddenly realizing how many women suffered in silence and the horrible toll it had to take on their lives. Her heart hurt hearing about it; she wanted to be of help to them all.

"I called the depression for what it was," Nessa continued, grimly. "In fact, I even told Sean what I thought."

Olivia found that interesting. "What did he say?"

"He just scoffed at me, wouldn't listen," Nessa answered. "This kind of thing doesn't happen to women in Sean's world. He kept telling Raine to try harder, look at the bright side of being a mother. She couldn't, though, it was too much for her. Finally, Sean seemed to get used to it."

Olivia was startled to hear this and upset that Sean hadn't mentioned it to her. Raine's depression could well be connected to why she'd fooled around with the stripper. To help her feel better about herself. Or to break out of the grip of sadness that had gripped her.

"I'm sorry to hear this, very sorry," said Olivia. "It sounds like Raine was trying to feel better about herself again."

"You mean by playing around with the stripper?" Nessa brushed her moist hair off her forehead then.

"That's public information?" Olivia bluntly asked.

"Of course it is," Nessa replied. "Among the girls, anyhow. I myself watched Raine all night long, kept trying to pull her back to her senses. I couldn't, of course. It was like watching a train wreck about to happen."

"Is that why she's disappeared?" asked Olivia. "Because she's upset and guilty about fooling around with him? Is she hiding from everyone?"

Nessa let out a strange laugh. "Raine wasn't upset or guilty about Luigi at all. She couldn't care less about the encounter. A moment of fun. What did it matter? What she was upset about was that she'd lost a lot of money."

"She paid him a lot?" Olivia felt herself getting cold again.

"No, not that." Nessa started walking toward the window and Olivia followed closely behind her. "Raine lost a bunch of money gambling at the casino."

"Recently?" Olivia asked.

"Over and over," Nessa whispered. "You know that Raine was a gambling addict, don't you?"

"An addict?" Olivia knew Raine used to enjoy gambling here and there back in college. When had it risen to the level of being an addict? Being out of control of herself?

"Yeah, Raine was addicted," Nessa repeated clearly.

Olivia shook her head slowly. "I had no idea."

"You hadn't seen her for a long while, had you?" Nessa rubbed her hands over the windowpanes.

"No, we lost touch," said Olivia.

"You didn't lose touch." Nessa turned and confronted her plainly. "Raine wrote you off because you never showed up at her wedding! In fact, she and I talked about it. I told her to give you a break. She wouldn't."

Olivia was about to defend herself and stopped. Raine's friends obviously knew all about her. It didn't matter what they thought. Olivia had to keep her focus on Raine for now.

Nessa suddenly looked spent, tired and saddened. "Why don't you go talk to Abby about Raine?" she suggested. "You need the big picture, something from everyone."

"Who's Abby?" Olivia was almost afraid of finding out more.

"Abby's another good friend. She's very different from me. Abby lives up in Coconut Grove, is married to a rich guy there."

"You're not close to Abby?" Olivia was curious.

"Not at all," said Nessa. "But Raine was close to both of us. Raine was funny like that, she had all kinds of friends, right across the spectrum. After the bachelorette party was over Raine went gambling that night and so did Abby. In fact, Abby was with Raine at the gambling table all night."

CHAPTER NINE

Before driving back up to Miami to speak to Abby, Olivia wanted to talk to Sean about Raine's condition. It was too late for him to hide anything from her now. It didn't make sense and Sean had to understand that.

Olivia put in a call to Sean right away. "Let's meet right now for a quick coffee," she said the moment he picked up.

"Sorry, I can't do that," Sean replied. "I'm about to leave for Miami. How about going over things back there?"

"I want to talk to you now," Olivia insisted.

"Look, I've got lots to take care of there and so do you," he balked. "The police are working on things well down here. I've been in touch with them. I know."

That didn't work for Olivia, though. She didn't want to wait to tell Sean what she'd discovered. Each person she spoke to became a building block for the next. And Olivia needed Sean to totally level with her before she spoke to Abby.

"It won't take long," Olivia pressed him.

"What's the urgency?" Sean answered fast.

Olivia was startled. "What's the urgency?" she echoed.

"I'm sorry, of course I realize," Sean backtracked. "Okay, I'll be at the coffee shop in your hotel in about ten minutes. Then I head back home."

*

It was easy for Olivia to gather her few things together and be ready to see Sean in ten minutes. True, he was the grieving husband and had a lot on his plate, including his child and Raine's mother, who was caring for her back home. Olivia understood why he needed to get back right away. She also realized that it was hard for him to listen to news about Raine. Part of him was still pretending it hadn't happened.

Olivia took a quick look in the mirror before she hurried downstairs. Dressed in a navy denim dress and a print scarf, she wore her hair loose around her face, her blue eyes shining. To her surprise, she looked and felt at least ten years younger than she had when she first came down on the case. Must be all the adrenaline pumping, she thought. And not knowing what was coming next.

44

Olivia threw her bags over her shoulder and went down to the coffee shop immediately. She had to set things straight with Sean. Everything had to be laid out on the table. There could be no hiding at all and games would not be allowed.

*

When Olivia walked into the coffee shop Sean was already there, sitting alone at a booth, looking entirely disgruntled.

"Hi," Olivia said, as she slipped into the booth opposite him.

"I still don't know why we have to have this talk this minute," he complained. "We could have caught up in Miami."

"Don't you want to hear what I learned from Nessa?" Olivia quickly replied.

"Of course I do, and you could tell me there, too," he objected. "My emails are piling up like crazy, asking where Raine is! And her father is also on the way down to our home."

"I'm sorry," Olivia answered, "but I have to come first right now. I'm on the case and you have to help me."

"I am, I will," Sean sputtered. "What did you find out from Nessa? Tell me."

"Nessa said Raine had a bad case of postpartum depression," Olivia stated abruptly. "She said Raine couldn't care for your daughter at all."

Sean's eyes flashed. "Nessa exaggerates, she dramatizes everything. I never knew what Raine saw in that woman or why in the world they were friends!"

"Really?" asked Olivia. "Are you saying that Raine was a good mother to your daughter?"

"I'm not saying that exactly," Sean shot back. "Raine had her moods like we all do, she had good moments, enjoying our daughter, playing with her."

"That's not enough, though, is it, Sean?" Olivia insisted.

"What do you want from me?" His face grew red. "What are you suggesting?"

"It sounds to me like Raine was going through rough times." Olivia downplayed it, so Sean would be able to hear her. She didn't want to bring up the drugs or gambling addiction yet, either. Olivia wasn't sure he actually knew all the details and it could certainly put him over the edge.

"I gathered that Raine was definitely battling with depression of some kind," Olivia went on.

"Who doesn't battle depression?" Sean looked at Olivia strangely then. "The Lord tells us the enemy will always accost us. When we're strong in prayer, we can win."

Olivia was momentarily speechless. On the face of it there was no way to respond.

"Of course prayer is needed," she replied finally, "and also professional help may be useful as well."

"I never said that wasn't true," Sean agreed. "We had Raine's moods well under control."

"Who is we?" asked Olivia instantly. "Was Raine seeing a therapist or psychiatrist?"

"No, not at all." Again Sean bristled. "Our physician prescribed an antidepressant for Raine. She took it once in a while. That is not something I wish to make public, of course."

"There's nothing shameful in taking an antidepressant," Olivia insisted.

"There is to me," Sean replied curtly.

"Was the antidepressant enough?" Olivia plunged forward.

Sean sat up starkly. "What are you getting at?" The waitress came to their table then, but Sean brushed her away. "Are you suggesting Raine left on her own volition because she was unhappy?"

"It's possible, isn't it?" Olivia remarked. She had to get Sean on board with reality.

"That's ridiculous," he answered heatedly then. "Raine had what other women only dream of. Our home is beautiful, our daughter the best! I've given her whatever she's asked for, including time to get away and do her photography."

"And she's been a good wife to you?" Olivia pressed him further.

"Absolutely," Sean insisted. "Raine isn't weak, she's tremendously strong. She helps with all the charity events sponsored by my organization, helps raise money, make calls. She makes a beautiful appearance in public. People in the community turn to us regularly for all kinds of things."

"How does she take all those demands on her?" asked Olivia.

"She likes it. Raine jumps in to help whenever she's needed," Sean answered briskly.

Olivia remembered that Raine liked to do a great deal at college as well. It was entirely possible that Nessa was creating a picture of Olivia that was skewed. Olivia had no reason to disbelieve Sean.

"Thank you for filling me in," she said.

"It's fine," he responded abruptly. "I don't mean to be rushed, but if that's all you want to know, I really want to leave now. What's next for you?"

"I'm going to talk to Abby in Coconut Grove," Olivia informed him.

"Very good, very good, Abby's a smart, settled woman. Much more dependable than Nessa ever will be. And don't think I'm not grateful, because I am. We'll talk more later on."

"Fine," Olivia said, as Sean got up quickly, grabbed his briefcase, and rushed out of the coffee shop. Olivia decided to stay a few minutes longer herself, though, and have a decent breakfast before hitting the road. The pictures of Raine that Nessa and Sean gave her contradicted each other. But Olivia knew that different parts of a person could only be expressed with certain people, not others. It sounded like Raine had played the role of dutiful wife the very best she could. It was possible Sean knew nothing of what else lay inside her. Olivia certainly didn't want to be the one to let him know, either. She would leave that to Wayne and Lorna.

Olivia beckoned over the waitress, ordered eggs, waffles, and hot coffee, and took a deep breath. There was no way she could be of any use to anyone if she didn't take good care of herself. As she sat there thinking about Sean and waiting for her food, her phone rang. Olivia immediately picked up.

"It's Wayne," the familiar voice on the other end said. "Just calling to see how it's going."

Olivia was delighted. It was so good to have someone to check in with, absolutely necessary.

"It's going all ways," Olivia replied quickly. "Do you have time to hear what I've learned so far?"

"Absolutely," said Wayne, "tell me everything."

"I met Nessa down at her scuba diving school and she said Raine was suffering from postpartum depression. She was high more often these days and also a gambling addict. Could be a way of dealing with her depression?"

"Could be," Wayne said. "Was she suicidal? That's the big question here. Did Raine take her own life?"

"I can't believe that she did," said Olivia. "I sure hope not."

"Of course," Wayne agreed, "but with depression, it's something we have to consider."

"What about you?" Olivia quickly turned it around. The idea that her friend had killed herself was more than she could handle. "Is there anything to add yet?"

"We also found out that Raine used drugs." Wayne was right on it. "There's no trail yet to any dealers, though. Lots of people use, so it's not the biggest clue. And yes, Raine also regularly frequented a casino nearby. No one referred to her yet as an addict, though."

Olivia was impressed at how much information Wayne had gathered in a short time.

"You and Lorna are doing a great job, Wayne," she said.

"I'm doing it, not Lorna," he replied. "Lorna's otherwise occupied at the moment."

"I'm sorry about that," said Olivia. "Lorna did say you guys had lots to handle."

"Yes, we have," Wayne agreed, "but this case is center and front for me. I'm giving it my all, Olivia."

"Thank you so very much." Olivia was touched.

"I have to. You've been through enough for one lifetime," he added.

Despite herself, Olivia smiled. "Way more than enough," she agreed.

"Let me fill you in on what else is going on here," Wayne continued. "We've got the posters printed, a search team organized, tip line set up, and also a line for ransom calls."

Olivia was amazed. "How great," she said.

"You're helping a lot by talking to Raine's close friends in depth and letting us know what you discover. I also plan to go back to the Sancho and talk to Luigi later tonight. You stay away from that place for now."

Olivia smiled; Wayne was sounding protective. "I will," she said.

"Actually, I was thinking it would be nice to meet for lunch so we can get on the same page with everything," Wayne suggested.

"I'm driving back up to Miami soon," Olivia remarked.

"Oh?" Wayne sounded disappointed. "Why?"

"I have to talk to some of Raine's other friends there," Olivia said. "Let's hold that lunch until I return."

"Well, if you're going, get started right away," Wayne said in response. "There a tropical storm all set to hit there tonight or tomorrow."

CHAPTER TEN

After breakfast, Olivia quickly checked her texts. There was one after another she hadn't read; it was to be expected. The texts were from Allison, her father, and the people at work. Olivia skimmed them briefly one after another. Allison and her father wanted to know her plans, where she was exactly, and how long she planned to stay. Fair enough, thought Olivia. She'd answer them when she arrived in Miami as best she could. Olivia would tell them where she could be reached, but how long she'd stay was open-ended.

The people at work had more specific questions. Was Olivia planning to come back and resume her position? Naturally, they had to know when as soon as possible. Olivia had already taken a leave of absence and she doubted they would extend it much further. She wasn't ready to completely cut ties at work, but she couldn't give them a time when she would return, either. She knew she wasn't going back soon, though. There wasn't much time left to firm it all up. Olivia hoped the right answer would come to her shortly.

Olivia left the coffee shop quickly, jumped into her car, and started to drive along the beautiful, scenic highway back up to Miami. As she drove beside the water, a sense of sadness gripped her. What was she doing here alone, wandering around amidst danger? Her father would certainly want an answer to that and he had every right to want it. It was a good question and Olivia didn't have an answer. How could she tell him or tell herself that she didn't feel fit any longer to live a normal life? The routines at work couldn't hold her. She'd seen too much, been through too much disappointment. There didn't seem to be anything up in New York for her. She wasn't looking for a new relationship either, probably wouldn't be for a long, long while.

Dark clouds started to gather as Olivia drove along. She was actually enjoying the day, strange as that might seem. She liked being on the road, digging deeper and deeper into things, exposing the truth. It was also fascinating to meet all kinds of new people, enter their worlds and extend a hand. Even though she and Raine had grown apart these past few years, Olivia felt their friendship was stronger than ever as she searched for her and found out about the challenges Raine had undergone.

As Olivia drove along, the wind picked up. Must be the storm coming, she thought. Sean had gotten her a room in a hotel in

Miami and she decided to go there first, shower and change before she headed over to see Abby.

*

By the time Olivia arrived in Miami, the skies were dark and the winds blowing harder. She pulled into her hotel to shower, change, and order up some food.

In a few minutes, as she was finishing the last bite of her sandwich, the hotel phone rang sharply, startling her. Could it be Sean checking in on her, Olivia wondered, or possibly Wayne?

She rushed to the phone and picked it up. A woman's voice was on the other end.

"Olivia, this is Abby. Just wondering if you returned from Miami yet."

"Yes, a little while ago," said Olivia promptly, appreciating the call. "I was planning to come to see you in a few minutes."

"Excellent," Abby replied. "I'm here waiting. I just was hoping you'd get here before people started arriving and we could be alone."

"I didn't realize that," Olivia said, flustered.

"No problem at all," Abby replied. "Just the sooner you get here the better."

"Absolutely." Olivia got the message. "I'll be on the road in a minute."

*

Coconut Grove was a few miles away from where Raine lived. One of Miami's oldest neighborhoods, founded by artists, intellectuals, and adventurers, it was a tropical oasis. It seemed to be Miami's escape from the stress of city life.

Olivia drove along the streets, completely charmed. Located in the middle of Miami, yet completely separate and quaint, there was a warm, laid-back atmosphere of unusual boutiques, sidewalk cafes, and sailboats that dotted the coastline.

After driving a few blocks Olivia turned down a quaint road to the address Abby gave her. She pulled up in front of a beautiful, wooden home surrounded by palm trees and flowers. Despite the growing wind and chill in the air, it was good to be here. Olivia got out, walked quickly to the front entrance, and hit the large wooden knocker on the door. In a few moments, a tall, willowy, exquisitely groomed young woman opened it.

50

"So glad you got here quickly," Abby breathed. "I can't take another minute of this. Not a minute."

"I can understand," said Olivia, calming her down.

Abby seemed to almost to be made of porcelain. Her short brown hair was perfect coiffed, framing her large doe eyes. Didn't seem like the kind to stay up all night gambling, thought Olivia.

"Come in immediately," Abby went on. "Phil's not home yet and it's better this way."

"Phil's your husband?" Olivia asked as she walked into the beautiful home, with wooden moldings, ceiling beams, and charming, personalized accents.

"Yes, he is," Abby answered quickly. "We've been married two years."

Olivia nodded, looking around. "Your home is magical," she offered.

"Thanks." Abby was happy to hear that. "I decorated it. Phil loves it as well. Actually, he needs it. He himself can be stuffy, but I'm the fresh breath of air in his life."

Olivia smiled. She liked Abby immediately; it was refreshing to be here with her.

"Phil's older than I am," Abby continued. "He's a bit settled in his ways."

Olivia was interested to hear that and surprised that Abby was sharing her life so readily.

"Look, I know this is not about me and Phil," Abby said then as she led Olivia into her large, white tile kitchen and pulled out a chair at the counter. "Please sit down here and I'll get you some coffee."

"I just had some," said Olivia. "Let's talk."

Relieved, Abby sat at the counter opposite her. "I heard that you know that I was with Raine at the casino the night of the party," she started.

Olivia was startled. "Word sure does get around. How do you know that? Nessa told you?"

"Yes, she did," said Abby. "Nessa called immediately after you left and told me all about you."

"You two are good friends?" Olivia wanted to check that again, hear what Abby had to say.

"Very," Abby answered without blinking an eyelash. "We're all, more or less, very good friends."

That was certainly not what Nessa had told Olivia. Olivia decided to say nothing about that at the moment.

"You don't want anyone to listen to our conversation," Olivia went forward immediately, "so I assume you have something secret to tell me?"

Abby blinked her eyes a few times and shook her head. "I wouldn't say secret, but personal," she replied. "There's definitely a difference."

"Yes, there is," Olivia agreed.

"I mean I don't need Phil finding out that I was with Raine gambling at the casino at the end of the party," Abby added.

"Of course not," Olivia went along.

"That's not the kind of thing Phil would take well to." Abby gave Olivia a quiet glance. "I'm sure you understand?"

"I do," said Olivia. "Do you go to the casinos often?"

"No, I don't, very seldom." Abby shook her head forcefully. "Raine does, though, all the time. She goes to both the one here in Miami and the one in Key West."

"Would you say she's addicted to gambling?" Olivia had to ask.

"I've thought that myself," Abby answered, noncommittally.

"Is Phil aware of that?" Olivia asked, wondering how he would like his pristine wife to spend time with a gambling addict.

"Of course he isn't," Abby retorted quickly. "And why should he be? What difference should it make to my husband what Raine does?"

"I just thought maybe you and Raine went out together with your husbands as couples?" Olivia asked.

"Yes, sometimes we do, of course," Abby commented. "In fact, our husbands happen to be good friends, and I can understand why. They're similar."

"How?" asked Olivia, electrified.

"They're both extremely successful, very particular." Abby closed her eyes slowly. "Both have strong views about how life must go."

Olivia found it interesting to hear that. "It can be hard to live with someone like that," she mentioned.

"It can be, doesn't have to, though," Abby said flippantly in return. "So of course Phil doesn't know much about Raine's private life. Phil's a banker, doesn't need to hear that Raine lost tons of money regularly."

"Really, tons of money?" Olivia's eyes grew wide.

"Yes, she was definitely in debt a lot of the time," Abby went on. "I told you Phil can be stuffy. If he found out, he might not have thought it was a good idea for me and Raine to be friends!"

52

"Do you lose money too?" asked Olivia quickly.

"No, hardly ever, I told you," Abby insisted, "I just went to the casino that night with Raine. She was high, she was woozy, and frankly, I didn't want her to be there alone."

"Why didn't you tell her that?" asked Olivia.

"I did, I begged her to go back to the hotel. She wouldn't listen, she was on a roll. Raine could get like that at times. Not always, but sometimes." Abby eyes started to fill with tears. "I'm terrified now about what happened to her! Absolutely terrified."

"Of course you are," Olivia breathed, beginning to feel terrified as well. "Does Sean know about Raine's gambling and debts?"

"I have no idea about that." Abby seemed to be feeling out of sorts now. "I never asked her about personal matters like that. She once told me that her debts did get paid somehow, so I left it at that."

"You never wondered how?" asked Olivia, amazed.

"Of course I wondered." Abby stood up now, uneasy. "But there's just so much I really wanted to know. I like Raine, I enjoy her company. We do all kinds of fun things together. The gambling was a part of her life that was her business!"

"But it's become our business now too," Olivia replied. "If she was indebted to someone and couldn't get the money to pay, that could be a clue to finding out where she is now."

"I know, I know." Abby broke down in tears then.

"What happened the night you spent with her at the casino?" Olivia zeroed in.

"Nothing unusual, I guess. She played the tables, drank a lot, lost money, laughed. People knew her there, she's a regular."

"I mean was there anyone there in particular interacting with her?" Olivia went on.

"No one in particular that I saw," Abby breathed.

Olivia thought Wayne should check out the casino, and that she should probably do it as well.

"Did you ever go to the casino here in Miami with Raine?" Olivia needed more details from Abby. Was the person she was indebted to located up here? Did they track Raine down to the casino in Key West that night?

"I went with her to the casino in Miami once or twice." Abby could barely speak now. "It was normal, nothing much. I could see, though, that as time passed, she became more and more frantic. She had to win. Became insistent upon it. Borrowed more and more when her luck started to run out."

Abby's words went through Olivia like a knife. Had Raine's luck run out now? Was her life over?

"Listen," Abby continued talking, "Raine's father, Edward, is on the way down. He's actually staying here at our place."

"Really? How come?" Olivia was interested. She vaguely remembered meeting Raine's father years ago at school. He was a tall, stately man, who'd been kind to both of them.

"Raine's father and mother just got through a bitter divorce," Abby quickly replied. "Her mother's seeing a much younger guy, and Edward's disgusted. He wants nothing to do with her. Raine's mom is staying at her house now, taking care of Raine's daughter."

"I heard that," said Olivia.

"It's a huge mess," Abby went on. "There's enough tension there anyway to rip out the moon."

Olivia took a deep breath.

"I think Raine's father would love to see you when he arrives," Abby went on. "It would be good for you too, to talk to him."

"Definitely," agreed Olivia.

"And then you've got to talk to both Miranda and Sloane," Abby continued, distraught now. "Somebody knows what's happened to her!"

"They're other friends at the party?" asked Olivia.

"Sloane is the bride-to-be." Abby was growing anxious. "She also lives in Miami and so does Miranda. Right now, Sloane's spending a lot of time at Raine's house, trying to help. Miranda was also at the party, constantly watching Raine's every move. I wondered why."

"I'll talk to both of them," Olivia assured her.

"Miranda's newly divorced and a bit different," Abby continued. "She keeps count of what everyone else has. Sometimes you get the feeling she'd rip it all away from you in a second if she could. That's another reason I decided to join Raine at the casino that night."

"You were afraid that Miranda would turn up there?"

"I didn't know. It was possible," said Abby. "Miranda turns up unexpectedly all the time. I felt uneasy around her, I'm telling you!"

"I hear you," said Olivia, as a harsh burst of rain began striking the windows.

"Oh my God, the storm is hitting," Abby said as she ran from one window to another, shutting them.

Olivia followed Abby, helping, and as they got to the front window, Olivia saw a long, dark car pull up and park.

"Who's that?" asked Olivia. "Phil?"

"It's not his car," breathed Abby. "It must be Raine's father, Edward. Oh my God, the storm has really begun! Where is Phil? Why is he late again?"

CHAPTER ELEVEN

Heavy winds and rain tossed against Raine's father as he got out of his car and pushed his way up Abby's driveway.

"Come in, Edward, come in!" Abby flung the door open, helping him inside.

"Crazy weather," he muttered, shaking off the rain.

"I'm so glad you got here before the worst of it." Abby gave him an embrace as if she were his own daughter.

"Thank you, sweetheart," Edward responded, then turned to look at Olivia.

"Do you remember me?" asked Olivia.

"Of course I do," he responded. "You were Raine's good friend and roommate at college."

"Yes, I was." Olivia was delighted that he knew who she was.

"I heard you'd become a private detective and are down here helping us, now," Raine's father said, looking a bit confused.

"I'm helping, of course," said Olivia, "but not exactly a private detective."

"Of course you are," Abby objected. "And you're doing a wonderful job. What's the difference between what you're doing and any private investigator Sean could have randomly hired?"

"Experience," Olivia started to say, but Abby stopped her.

"It's better to have someone who knew Raine and the family than someone who couldn't care less about what happened to her."

"Okay, enough of this!" Edward raised his hands. "What actually is going on? Tell me! What kind of game is Raine playing now?"

"We're not sure yet." Abby's eyes filled with tears. "You'd be better off talking to Olivia."

Edward looked at Olivia through suddenly bleary eyes. "I'd be glad to do that, naturally."

"I'll give you two your privacy," Abby said then, as she whirled around, eager to take her leave.

"There's no need for you to go," Edward called out after her. "I have no secrets!"

"It's better this way," Abby called back, obviously eager to be someplace else.

When Abby had left, Edward turned back to Olivia. "Abby's a sensitive type, always has been. She can only take so much of life. Her husband makes up for it, though. They've made a good match. He's got both feet planted solidly on the ground."

"So I heard," said Olivia.

"What else did you hear?" Edward was becoming more focused now. "Let me have it! What exactly is going on with my daughter?"

The way he said it, Olivia wondered if this was something they'd been through before.

"I need to know what you think happened," Olivia responded quickly. "Tell me more about Raine. Why do you think she might be playing this game with us?"

"Do you have all night?" Edward responded and smiled bitterly as he ushered Olivia into the living room and sat down on a plush sofa with her.

"I have as long as it takes," Olivia replied.

"You're a good woman, Olivia," Edward murmured, touching Olivia deeply. "That's hard to find these days."

"Thank you," Olivia replied. It felt good to hear that.

"Okay, where do I start now?" Edward went on. "I'm sure you've heard by now that my daughter had a gambling addiction?"

"I've heard that several times," Olivia replied.

"Her gambling craze has actually been going on a long time," Edward continued. "It started pretty soon after she married Sean."

Olivia was surprised to hear that.

"In the beginning she was good at hiding it," Edward continued. "I told myself it was the hunger for excitement Raine was born with. Even when she was little she needed all kinds of thrills. You couldn't just leave her alone with nothing planned. As soon as she married Sean and then found the casinos that hunger grabbed her big time."

Olivia found it frightening listening to him.

"Raine always waiting for the big kill!" Edward was becoming upset. "She was sure she'd win millions. I said to her time and again, so what if you win millions? What are you going to do with them? She'd laugh and say it didn't matter! She just had to win! But she didn't. She lost big time, actually."

Olivia found the story both gripping and painful.

"Raine lost again and again and wouldn't face it." Edward's face grew flushed. "She always said next time things would turn around! Her big stash was waiting right around the corner."

"It wasn't, though," Olivia echoed.

"Of course not. Never! Finally she started to promise me she'd stop gambling soon. I was the stupid one to believe her. In the beginning I paid her debts."

"It doesn't mean you were stupid, it means you were kind." Olivia felt terrible for Edward.

"No, kind would have been to get her into rehab!" Edward declared forcefully. "Kind would have been to recognize that my daughter was up against an illness! This was more than a search for thrills. She was trapped inside a vicious compulsion."

Olivia was impressed with Edward's honesty.

"But instead, I kept paying through the nose." Edward's voice started to grow jagged. "Then I had enough. After all, she was married to Sean. She belonged to him, not me. She was his responsibility, not mine. Even though she kept asking me to pay, suddenly I refused. Let Sean pay your debts now, I told her."

"How did Raine react to that?" Olivia could only imagine.

Edward guffawed. "She couldn't believe her ears. She kept coming back and asking again, thinking I'd change my mind. I didn't, though. She was Sean's at this point."

"Did Sean know about her addiction?" Olivia wondered how all this had affected him.

"It seems he didn't," Edward remarked. "The first time Raine asked him to pay, Sean got furious. He absolutely refused. It was a small debt, too. I told him he was a no-good, rotten husband. He said he couldn't care less what I thought. He wasn't going to pay gambling debts for anyone. As far as I know Raine never asked him again."

"He didn't know her gambling had turned into an addiction?" Olivia needed to be clear on this point.

"As far as I know he didn't," Edward answered. "But how can I be certain? He'd barely talk to me after that."

"My God," breathed Olivia, "what happened? Who paid her debts?"

"That's the question that torments me, too," Edward continued. "When I once asked Sean about it again, he wouldn't answer. If you ask me, that guy doesn't have a heart. Neither does Raine. Once I stopped paying her debts, I became yesterday's news."

Olivia was horrified.

"Of course I kept check on my daughter in my own way." Edward seemed to feel good finally talking about it. "Her gambling kept going, so somebody had to be coughing up the dough. I even know who her current lender is now."

"Who?" asked Olivia instantly.

"A guy named Alan Dupris," Edward answered. "Dupris's a big player in the casino world. Holds lots of debts. Has big connections."

"This is important information," breathed Olivia, "very."

"I'm sure it is." Edward seemed agitated. "Pass it along. If anyone knows where Raine is hiding, it's Dupris."

"Does Sean know Dupris?" Olivia asked.

"Good question," said Edward. "But that's anyone's guess, isn't it? Sean can't stand me now, will barely talk to me. If I had my way I'd break up that marriage. My daughter deserves much better than him."

This was the first time Olivia had heard anything unpleasant about Sean. It was from an irate father-in-law, though. Olivia had to remind herself that what Edward said wasn't necessarily true. The relationship had to be trying for Sean, as well.

"I heard that Raine also had a rough time caring for your granddaughter?" Olivia wanted to hear anything else Edward had to add.

"Yeah, that's the way they like to put it," Edward snapped. "Raine's lousy mother keeps calling and telling me that. But if you asked me, I'd say Raine's rough time was with Sean! When a woman's happy in her marriage, it's easy to be a mom, isn't it?"

"I wouldn't know," said Olivia sadly.

"Yeah, I heard you've been through a lot," Edward answered, suddenly sad. "I'm really sorry."

"Thank you," said Olivia.

"But it's true, isn't it?" Edward repeated. "When a woman is getting all the love she needs from her husband, it's easy to give their baby love."

"Maybe it is and maybe it isn't," Olivia replied. "I'm not an expert, but I have heard that postpartum depression is triggered by all kinds of things."

"Nah," Edward went on. "I blame it all on Sean. And there's one thing more I want to say to you. Don't probe too much into everything. Raine will be back by herself soon. And I don't want her reputation to get ruined in the meantime."

A sudden flash of lightning lit up the sky then, accompanied by a clap of thunder. The very next moment Abby flew into the room.

"It's all out there on the news," Abby cried. "I just saw it. They're showing pictures of Raine and asking for anyone who has seen her to contact the police immediately. Oh my God! This is real, it's happening!"

Olivia wished she could have seen the broadcast.

"What are you going to do, Olivia?" Abby went on. "Go to Sean's house now? Or stay here with us until the rain lets up?"

As the rain poured harder, Olivia's phone suddenly lit up with a text from Wayne. The timing couldn't be more perfect, she thought.

Where are you? Have to speak to you! On my way up to Miami tonight. Let's get together and debrief first thing tomorrow!

What did he want to talk to her about? He must have found something.

Great. Tomorrow morning is perfect, Olivia texted back.

Abby slipped up close behind Olivia. "Why not stop in for a few minutes at Sean's before you go back to the hotel?" she repeated. "I'm sure it would help them to have you there."

It had been a long day and Olivia wanted to get back to her hotel. She'd already spoken with Sean that morning.

"Sloane's there, too," Abby added. "Just drop in and say hello to her. Let her know you're working the case."

Olivia paused for a moment. There was an urgency about Abby's request that didn't go unnoticed. "Okay, I'll call them now and tell them I'm coming," she replied.

"No, don't call." Abby bristled. "Just go drop in on them. It's a better idea."

*

Olivia drove in the pouring rain to Sean's home through streets that were mostly empty. When she pulled up at the driveway, to her surprise, the house seemed dark and forbidding. The lights were barely on and the rain pounded harshly on the rooftop.

Olivia slipped out of her car and fled through the wind up to the front entrance. She rang the bell fiercely several times before a voluptuous young woman with long, thick golden brown hair and huge dark eyes answered. The young woman looked out the door, alarmed.

"Who's there?" she uttered.

"Olivia Wells," Olivia answered as the young woman kept staring at her.

"Can I come in?" Olivia had to ask.

The young woman opened the door slightly and Olivia rushed in out of the rain.

"For a second I thought it was Raine," the young woman breathed. "We're not expecting anyone else now."

This had to be Sloane, thought Olivia. "Are you Sloane?"

"Yes, I am. Who told you?" Sloane's eyes fluttered. "Why are you here?"

"I thought I could be of help," said Olivia.

"Come back tomorrow, not now," Sloane spoke rapidly. "It's been a hard afternoon and things are just settling down. Raine's mom has finally gotten Clea to sleep. She's in the den now, resting. Sean is answering one email after another."

"I can only imagine," breathed Olivia.

Sloane seemed to calm down a bit then. "There's nothing for you to do here now anyway," she assured Olivia.

"It's good of you to stay here with everybody," said Olivia.

Sloane shrugged it off. "Where else would I be?" she answered. "This happened because of my party!"

Olivia wanted to say it wasn't her fault, but held back any comment. Sloane was interesting and she wanted to learn more about her.

"Call tomorrow morning," Sloane suggested then. "Everyone will be more rested. It's a better time."

"Fine," Olivia agreed. Then, as an afterthought, she turned back to Sloane. "Can I give you a lift back home? It's hard driving out there."

"No thanks." Sloane tossed her long hands in front of her face impatiently, as if pushing Olivia away. "It's enough, go home. I'm staying here tonight, anyway."

"Really? Why?"

Sloane was offended. Her eyes opened wide. "Why not?" she answered, briskly. "They need me here. You have a problem with it? Too bad for you."

CHAPTER TWELVE

Back in her hotel room Olivia quickly called Wayne to make arrangements for tomorrow morning. She couldn't shake the strange feeling she'd had from meeting Sloane, though. After she and Wayne set a time for the next day, Olivia mentioned it.

"It's not that I have an actual problem with Sloane," said Olivia, "it's just that the house had a dark, hollow feeling, as if something terrible had happened there."

"Of course it has," Wayne answered. "Why wouldn't it? Someone has gone missing from it. Reality is hitting, fear is rising. It's to be expected. It's best for you to get some rest now. You've had an incredibly long day. The storm's supposed to let up in a few hours. The flights should be back up without any problem. Before you know it, I'll be there. You don't have to handle all this alone."

When they hung up the phone Olivia felt incredibly grateful for Wayne's help. Of course, she couldn't do this alone. And she didn't have to. She finally felt like part of a team, doing something that mattered more than anyone could say. A rush of respect and admiration for Wayne and the work hit her. Olivia knew she had to contact the folks back at work and let them know when she was returning. There was no way she could leave in the middle of this, though. That much she knew at least. A big decision lay in front of her and she was eager to speak with Wayne first and hear what he had to say!

*

When Olivia awoke the next morning, the storm had subsided. As she looked out of her hotel window, the aftereffects were scattered helter-skelter on the ground. Broken twigs, branches, and assorted objects were strewn everywhere. Thankfully the storm was over now and Wayne would arrive soon. Once again, Olivia wondered exactly why he was coming to Miami. She was eager to find out and also to tell him all she'd discovered up to now.

Olivia dressed slowly, choosing a lime green flowered dress, open white sandals, and a necklace of hand-painted seashells, delicately strung together. She loved wearing beautiful colors and prints. It lifted her spirits, fortified her. Often it felt like a defense against the upcoming struggles of the day.

Just as Olivia put the last touches on her makeup, Wayne called to say he was on the way. He would pick her up in the lobby in a few minutes. Olivia was glad to hear that, looked forward to seeing him again.

She went right down to wait in the lobby and in a little while Wayne walked in. When Olivia saw him, she was taken aback. Wayne was dressed in a navy sports jacket, his usually tousled hair perfectly brushed back from his face. Filled with energy, focus, and purpose, he almost looked as though he'd stepped off the cover of a magazine.

"Good to see you," was the first thing Wayne said as he approached Olivia. "You look terrific today. Detective work must be agreeing with you."

"Thanks," Olivia answered lightly, thinking exactly the same thing about him.

"Let's go now." Wayne was right on it. "I've got the car waiting out front and have made reservations at LaPlaine. It's a fun restaurant near the beach where we won't be rushed."

Olivia smiled briefly as she walked quickly beside him out of the hotel and into his car.

"How's it going?" she asked as the car pulled out into the street.

"It's going. I'll tell you more when we get there," he said as he started to wind in and out between traffic.

"Slow down a little," Olivia suggested. "We want to get there in one piece."

Wayne smiled. "I've got a bunch of things lined up for the trip. I want to get there as fast as I can so we have as much time as needed for brunch."

*

LaPlaine was a five-star restaurant, situated close to the shore. The place was both high end and filled with beachfront simplicity. As soon as Olivia and Wayne entered, they were directed to a table in the front, overlooking both gardens and sand.

"What a beautiful spot," said Olivia, looking at the large array of hanging plants. Music was piped in and a television in the far corner, a bit away from them, was on with the news of the day.

"I've been here a few times," said Wayne as they took their seats. "The food's terrific too."

"Thanks for all your help, Wayne," Olivia offered.

"No, thank *you*," he responded as they picked up their menus. "You're a real trouper and I appreciate it."

After ordering, they relaxed a bit and looked at each other. A soft ocean breeze that blew in from the open window was both refreshing and comforting. Olivia still felt a bit nervous being here with Wayne, though. Everything was different now.

"Okay, you go first," Wayne started. "Tell me what you've got so far."

Olivia was relieved to jump right in. "I talked to Abby, a good friend of Raine's, and also to Raine's father. Raine definitely had developed a gambling addiction. It's been going on for a while, too."

Wayne listened attentively.

"It seems that originally, Raine's father paid her gambling debts," Olivia continued. "Then he had enough and wanted Sean to take them over."

"And did he?" asked Wayne, fascinated.

"From what I heard Sean refused. I'm not sure he knew about the addiction, though, and also not sure who has been picking up Raine's tab since then."

"It's urgent that we find this out," Wayne commented. "If not Sean, who could it be? And also, who does she owe money to?"

"Her current lender is a man named Alan Dupris," Olivia promptly reported.

"Dupris, Dupris, I've heard that name," Wayne muttered.

"He's a big player in the casino world," Olivia continued.

"That's it! Exactly! You're good, Olivia, you're fantastic." Wayne began to take notes as she spoke. "We'll get right on this guy immediately. What else?"

"I stopped briefly at Sean's house last night, as I told you on the phone," Olivia continued. "Raine's mother was there, along with Raine's friend Sloane, the bride-to-be."

"You mentioned that you felt strange about Sloane last night, as I recall?" Wayne said.

"Yes, I did," said Olivia, glad that he remembered. "She's beautiful, like the rest of them, but she seemed extremely nervous. Actually, she couldn't get me out of there fast enough."

"Why?"

"Good question," said Olivia. "It was late, pouring rain, and Sloane said Raine's mother had just gotten the child to sleep and was resting in the den. Sean was poring over emails, and it would be better to talk to them in the morning."

"Did you?" asked Wayne.

"No, not yet," said Olivia. "I wanted to talk to you first."

"Good," Wayne replied. "I've also been researching the family. Seems there's a lot of bad blood between Raine's mother and Sean. The mother's supposed to be really off-beat. She has a much younger boyfriend and Sean can't stand her. He's embarrassed about it. He's a pretty uptight guy."

"Why else do they have all this bad blood?" Olivia asked.

"I believe Sean was a wedge between Raine and her mother. Kept them apart. When the baby was born and Raine had all that trouble, Sean had no choice but to call the mother for help. He needed her then."

Olivia made a sour face as the waiter brought their food and laid it down before them. Both of them looked at their plates, but neither took a bite.

"It's an old story with in-laws," Wayne continued. "Happens all the time. I don't think it amounts to much of anything."

Wayne spoke with such authority that Olivia wondered if he'd ever been married. There was no ring on his finger now, so she also wondered if he'd ever been divorced.

"You didn't happen to have a rough mother-in-law yourself?" Olivia asked, suddenly playful.

Wayne laughed unexpectedly. "Never got quite that far," he said, with a flashing smile. "After Kalie and I got engaged, her mother pulled out all the stops. She made things a living hell for us and Kalie buckled to everything her mom wanted."

"Her mother broke you up?" Olivia was aghast. "That must have been hard for you."

Wayne rubbed his forehead. "Actually, it was good. I thought it would be awful, but it wasn't. Once it was over I was relieved and tremendously grateful to have seen what I did about Kalie before we walked down the aisle."

"Sounds like you dodged a bullet," said Olivia.

"I'd certainly say so," Wayne replied.

Olivia was glad to know more about Wayne's personal life. "Thanks for sharing this with me," she said.

"Sure thing," Wayne replied. "It's easy to talk to you. And besides, I know what you've just been through with Todd."

Olivia felt a sense of sorrow suddenly come over her at the mention of Todd's name.

Wayne looked at Olivia oddly. "I wouldn't be so sad about him, either, if I were you. He's definitely not worth it. We've recently found out much more about him."

Olivia bristled, upset by Wayne's comment. "Todd's just lost his life," she responded crisply. "Whatever he did, he paid the price for it."

"Todd's life left a lot of people hurt and scarred." Wayne seemed compelled to speak. "In the past few days, Rhonda decided to spill the beans."

"Rhonda's trying to defend herself," Olivia retorted.

"Sure she is," Wayne answered swiftly. "But everything she's told us has checked out. Not only was Todd two-timing you, he did it in the past to lots of women. The guy left a trail of broken hearts and empty pocketbooks behind."

Olivia suddenly felt heartsick. "A professional con?"

"I would say so," Wayne replied, "but don't be too hard on yourself. The best and brightest women get taken in by con men all the time. The ones with the kindest hearts."

That didn't make Olivia feel any better. It was almost impossible to relate her experience of Todd to what she'd found out about him since he'd died. The disparity made her doubt herself and her perceptions. Had she been living her life half blind, lost in some kind of fantasy? Doing the work she was engaged in now, looking for clues, searching people's motives and listening carefully to what everyone said, made her feel more grounded. It began to correct her confusion about Todd.

"Todd was also involved in a smuggling scheme," Wayne continued. "He was stealing from people and stashing the money in weird places. No question, he was definitely some kind of psychopath."

Olivia's heart started beating harder. This was certainly not what she wanted to hear. "Okay, but he's gone now, it's over," she insisted.

"It's not over until you let it be." Wayne wouldn't let it go. "You've got to see the whole picture. You're still carrying a torch for the guy. It's all over your face when I mention his name. You're still hanging on, grieving. But please, don't waste another precious second of your life thinking of him."

Wayne was keen and perceptive and Olivia couldn't pretend everything he said wasn't spot on.

"Go take a bite of brunch," Wayne encouraged her. "You're doing great, you're down here working a case and the truth is, you're indispensable! We need you here, Olivia. If you wanted to, with a little training, you could easily join us on the force."

Olivia was startled to hear that. "Really?"

"I can't see why not," Wayne repeated.

But did Olivia want that? Was this life for her for the long run?

"Thank you, Wayne," she murmured. "But I'm not at all sure what's coming next."

"Okay, eat your brunch," he insisted as he took a bite of his. "There's a lot for both of us to handle right here, right now. After you first talk to all of the women at Raine's party, I'm going to meet each one briefly. After that, I'll bring them all down to Key West to talk to them all on the record."

"Is that why you came up to Miami?" Olivia asked.

"That and several other reasons. I'm hot on the money trail and have to talk both to Sean and to some people at the casino up here. If you want you can come with me."

"I do want to. I'd like that," said Olivia. "

"Great." Wayne was pleased. "After brunch I have a quick meeting, then we'll go to the casino together. I'll talk to Dupris and other money people there. You can talk to those who knew Raine as a regular and find out more about her. I also came up to talk to Raine's mother and see what she can add."

"How about Lorna?" Olivia couldn't help but ask. "Where is she?"

"Funny that you ask that," Wayne replied. "Right now she's joined one of the search teams out in the field. Lorna's also been busy posting pictures, organizing locals to join in, and arranging other ways to get the word out."

"She's a great partner," Olivia commented.

"In her own way she definitely is," Wayne responded, as suddenly the sound of the TV in the corner grew louder.

"Breaking news!" the announcer boomed and the screen flashed. *"Search teams are out searching for a beautiful, young Miami mother who's gone missing in Key West."* The reporter's tone was urgent.

"Oh my God, look at that." Olivia stood up to see better. "News about Raine!"

Wayne jumped up as well. "Great," he said, thrilled to see it. "I did everything I could to get this on the air."

"Search teams are spread out all over, searching for the victim," the reporter went on.

Photos of Lorna with others plowing through lowlands and bush then came up on the screen.

"There's Lorna!" Olivia exclaimed.

"Tough woman," Wayne commented. "If anyone can find anything she will."

To Olivia's amazement, next came a close-up of a reporter talking to Sean. This must have been shot when he was up in Miami. Sean looked exhausted and teary-eyed, barely was able to answer the questions being thrust at him.

"Exactly who was the last to see your wife alive?" the reporter asked a couple of times.

"She's still alive! We know it," Sean insisted in a faltering tone. "We're calling for prayers for Raine at the vigil back at our church in Miami soon. Please pray for Raine wherever you are!"

"Did you know about the vigil?" Olivia quickly asked Wayne.

"Yes, that's another reason I'm down here. I want to find out exactly who is attending."

"What do you want to say to your wife, if she's still out there?" the reporter asked Sean hurriedly.

68

"Raine, come home." Sean's voice broke. "We love you, we need you! Clea's waiting for you."

Completely choked up, he then fumbled away, practically incoherent, unable to say another word.

CHAPTER THIRTEEN

Olivia stood there feeling extremely uneasy as she watched the TV. She'd never seen Sean so upset or out of control.

"This is not the Sean I know," she said to Wayne.

"Raine's missing and it's becoming a reality," Wayne replied. "He's overwhelmed."

"I'm surprised he never told me about the vigil, either," Olivia went on. "It's on TV. Everyone else knows about it!" exclaimed Olivia.

"You don't have to go to the vigil if you don't want to," Wayne commented, soothingly. "I'll be there."

Olivia was relieved. There were so many bases to cover, she couldn't be everywhere. And she didn't want to meet Raine's mom at the vigil, either. Her dad would be there, too. Olivia liked Raine's dad and the entire situation would be too upsetting.

"I appreciate that," she said to Wayne as they both fell silent then, finishing up their meal quickly. "I have to pick my battles. It's too much all at once."

"Of course it is," Wayne replied. "In fact, I've been wondering how long you could even stay down here. What's going on with your job back at home? How much time are they giving you off?"

"It's a good question," said Olivia, "and I don't have an answer. They're not about to give me much more time. In fact, they're demanding I let them know if I'm even returning at all."

Wayne's eyes opened wide. "Really?" he exclaimed. "Are you thinking of leaving your job?"

"I am," said Olivia, surprising herself. "I returned for a short while and it was suffocating."

Wayne stopped drinking his coffee and listened.

"I felt trapped, confined, part of a world that had no more meaning to me," Olivia added, also putting her coffee cup back on the table.

"Todd's death turned your world upside down," Wayne commented.

"Yes, it did," agreed Olivia. "First meeting him turned my world upside down, and then his sudden murder. But it wasn't just his death, either, it's all the things I found out about him since."

"Hard to take, for sure," Wayne reflected.

Olivia was surprisingly glad to be talking about this to Wayne. "More than hard," she went on. "It makes me question everything about how I see people. Who they are really, and who I am."

"I certainly can understand that," Wayne agreed. "Those are important questions. I ask myself them almost every day of my life."

Olivia was delighted that Wayne resonated so deeply.

"So what's next?" Wayne took his credit card out of his pocket then to pay the bill.

"That's the question, isn't it?" Olivia commented.

"Yes, it is. And don't be in a hurry to answer it, either," said Wayne. "If you're not going back to work, why not stay down here for a while with us? See how you like it. For all you know this work could really fill the bill."

"Is that how it happened for you?" asked Olivia.

"No, for me it was instantaneous," Wayne said without hesitation. "I'm a guy who requires justice. From the time I was a kid I always wanted to be a detective. There was nothing else I ever wanted to do."

"That's lucky," said Olivia.

"More than lucky," Wayne commented. "This work is a blessing for everyone! Both the detectives and the devastated victims of crime."

*

After brunch was over and Wayne left for his meeting, Olivia had some time to spare. She decided to take a few moments alone to walk at the beach. The day was warm and the air clear after the storm. She had a longing to feel her feet on the damp sand.

As soon as she got down to the beach, Olivia took off her shoes and made her way down to the ocean. Whenever Olivia was upset or confused there was nothing like the ocean to make her feel settled and grateful just to be there, breathing alongside it.

As Olivia stood looking out into the horizon, thoughts of Raine filled her mind. How long would this search go on? Had Raine vanished of her own will? Had she just decided to chuck it all and run away? Was she still alive? Olivia looked down at the sand then and picked up a seashell that lay at her feet. It was perfectly shaped and beautiful, as Raine had been. What happened to her? The urgency to know was increasing quickly. Had Raine taken her own life due to depression? The thought that Raine might be dead was horrifying. Still, Olivia had to take it into consideration. Anything was possible at this point. Anything at all.

Olivia turned and started to walk along the edge of the water. How likely was it that Raine had come to harm? Was there someone who hated her, or wished her ill? Had Raine done something terrible to offend someone? Speaking with her friends, it didn't seem so. They all had nothing but praise for her. But who knew how truthful they were all being? Who knew what was lurking deep inside their hearts?

The waves played with Olivia's feet as she walked. It was good being down here, near the surf and sky. It was also fascinating to join the search for Raine. Olivia was finally doing something that felt real.

She stopped walking suddenly and sat down on the sand. Wayne had asked her good questions about her future. He was smart and perceptive, no doubt about that. By now Olivia needed to give answers. She couldn't go along like this in no-man's-land.

For starters, Olivia realized that she had come back down to Key West to find answers about her own life, as well as Raine's. She'd also needed to work out her feelings about Todd. But something larger was happening as well. Olivia was feeling useful, alive, and appreciated, operating on all cylinders. That was something she'd never felt in her entire life. She had suddenly fallen into a lifestyle that seemed completely suited to her. At least for now. She was definitely far from making any permanent decisions. But Olivia also could not delay answering the emails from back home at work.

Olivia reached into her bag, pulled out her cell phone, and without a moment's hesitation, wrote an email and then with the click of a finger, sent it off.

Sorry it's taken me so long to reply to you. I hope you will understand, but it doesn't seem as if I can return to my job at this time. I just can't do it anymore. Too much has happened. Thank you for being so considerate during this confusing time. It's been wonderful working with you.

After Olivia sent off the email, she stared out at the rollicking sea. What would her friends and family say when they heard the news? In just the flash of a second, she'd given up a life and job she'd loved and worked hard for. For a moment Olivia felt completely unanchored, having no idea what was coming next. The next minute she felt centered and certain. Joyous even. She was being called to something and she felt it. She didn't have to know exactly what it was either, right now.

Relieved that the decision had been made, Olivia got up from the sand, brushed herself off. There was time before she and Wayne went to the casino. Olivia decided to briefly stop in at Sean's house to see how they were all doing. She was ready to meet Raine's mother now too, and anyone else who might be there.

*

Olivia drove back to Sean's house quickly, invigorated from her time on the beach. She also felt freer having made a choice about work. Olivia could be here wholeheartedly now. She would let the next steps lead her where they did.

When Olivia pulled up in front of Sean's house, she was surprised to see Wayne's car outside as well. It was fine, she thought. After the big announcement on the news Sean would most likely be delighted to have all the support he could get.

Olivia rang the doorbell quickly, and to her surprise Sloane answered again.

Olivia registered her surprise. "Still here?" she asked.

"Why shouldn't I be?" Sloane sounded put off.

"I didn't mean it like that," Olivia said, edging into the house through the open door. "I just meant it must be hard for you being here so many hours."

"It's harder for Raine," Sloane answered in a throaty voice. "Wherever she is, this has to be harder for her. And for the rest of the people who love her."

Olivia couldn't dispute that. "Of course, you're right. I saw the newscast and Sean looked completely wrecked."

"Sean is strong." Sloane immediately defended him. "He'll pull through this, if anyone will. I'll see to it that he does!"

Olivia was taken aback by the intensity of her feeling. "He'll pull through because of you?"

"Sean will pull through because he loves his daughter and he's the kind of dad who would never let her down," Sloane added defensively.

Sloane looked at Olivia unwaveringly. She was certainly a person Olivia needed to know better.

"We'll have to talk more soon," Olivia said to her.

"Yes, we will, but not right now," Sloane hedged, once again. "By the way, your partner's here, too. He's been talking to Raine's mom, Barna."

Olivia wondered who Sloane meant by her partner. Then she realized she must be referring to Wayne.

"Wayne's not my partner." Olivia set the record straight. "I'm working directly for Sean."

"Really? Wayne referred to you as his partner." Sloane's eyebrows rose.

"Wayne probably meant I was someone on the case with him," Olivia corrected her again. "Wayne has a partner, Lorna."

"So where is Lorna then?" asked Sloane. "If you're a person's partner you're with them when they need you. Otherwise the word means nothing!"

Sloane had a blunt way of putting things. "I'd love to talk to Raine's mom now if I could." Olivia wanted to get off the topic.

"Barna's been busy talking to Wayne, your partner," Sloane repeated. "And she's thoroughly exhausted by everything. Wayne will tell you whatever she said. It's better to leave her alone for now. Listen, don't waste your time here now anyway. There are plenty of people around. If you want to talk to someone, go three blocks south and talk to Miranda."

"Why Miranda?" asked Olivia.

"Miranda's a very close friend of Raine's. They see each other all the time." Sloane seemed insistent. "And Miranda's the only one who saw Raine the next morning after the party, before she disappeared."

"What are you talking about?" Olivia was shocked. "I didn't realize that! Nobody does."

"But it's true anyway and I know it," Sloane whispered.

"This is important information. You shouldn't hide it."

"I didn't hide it. I just told it to you, didn't I?" Sloane looked away.

"Yes, you did and I thank you for it." Olivia was rattled.

"So, go talk to Miranda now. I'd go with you, but I have to help with Raine's daughter. I adore that child completely, always have. In fact, people are saying I'm practically a mother to her now."

Sloane's words disturbed Olivia. "But her grandmother is here, too."

"Yes, of course, but Barna's older, she's tired. I'm stepping in, big time. Clea needs someone, doesn't she?"

"Of course she does and I'm sure Sean appreciates that very much," breathed Olivia.

"More than you can imagine," Sloane assured her. "And so do I."

Sloane gave Olivia Miranda's contact information and Olivia turned to leave, when Wayne swiftly came up behind her.

"What are you doing here? Where are you going now?" Wayne asked, startled to see Olivia.

"I came to talk to Barna," Olivia replied. "I heard you just did that."

"That's right," said Wayne. "She's resting now. In fact, I was just about to call you. I'm on my way to the casino. I've got a few good leads there. Let's go."

"Okay, let's do it," said Olivia, planning to see Miranda right after that.

CHAPTER FOURTEEN

The Mayfair Casino in Miami spread over two, long blocks. Well known and heavily attended, the casino had big potted palms standing in front of it, along with flashing lights.

"It's important to check in here," Wayne said to Olivia as they pulled up. "I have a forensic accountant checking all Raine's accounts. He pointed me to a few people at the casino. Always follow the money, I say. You can't go wrong."

Olivia appreciated Wayne sharing his strategy with her. She felt included.

"It's equally important to follow Raine's personal life, dig up everything we can find out about her," Wayne continued. "Just the slightest slip by someone can open everything up."

Olivia wondered whether she should tell Wayne what she just found out about Miranda, but decided to wait until she spoke to her first.

"Someone either wanted Raine's money, her heart, or her life!" Wayne continued. "Raine could have hurt someone a lot, or else wouldn't pay up on a big debt."

"That's summing it up," Olivia answered.

Wayne nodded. "Of course, nothing can be summed up in a nutshell. The pieces come from all over the place. We're also finally getting some calls on the tip line."

"Like what do you hear?" Olivia was eager to find out.

"Someone called and said he'd spotted Raine in South Beach," Wayne continued.

"South Beach?" Olivia got excited. "That's not far from here. Raine's still around! Let's go." Olivia was thrilled. She couldn't wait to get there.

"Hold on." Wayne held up one hand. "We've got officers checking it out. Don't get excited, you always get all kinds of sightings and reports. Most of them amount to nothing. People want to feel they're part of the story."

"I'm still hopeful," Olivia said.

"Don't be," Wayne instructed. "If Raine's there, we'll find her. But don't count on it. It's not good to get excited. You get too disappointed then. Slow and steady is the best. Do all you can and expect nothing, is the best way."

Olivia wondered why Wayne was so afraid of getting excited and hoping for the best. What had disappointed him so much? But

Olivia wasn't going in that direction. She wasn't ready to give up hope.

"Raine could be close by, walking around," she murmured.

"I doubt it myself," Wayne responded.

"Why?" asked Olivia, her heart suddenly aching to see her friend again.

"If Raine's walking around, she would have seen us searching for her on the news and gotten in touch immediately. If she left on her own, she's far from here by now." Wayne was laying it all out, methodically. "If she was taken for ransom, they've got her well hidden." Then he stopped talking abruptly.

"What else?" Olivia pressed, as the car came to a halt in front of the casino and he parked.

"If Raine's killed herself, we may never find her at all," Wayne went on. "She could be at the bottom of the sea. If someone else killed her, we have to find out who and why!"

"That about sums it up." Olivia was shuddering. Wayne's words were so cut-and-dried, she couldn't accept them. A person's whole life couldn't be reduced to a few possibilities.

"There are no other scenarios?" she asked.

"Can you think of one?" said Wayne.

"Raine might have had an accident?" Olivia speculated. "She was high, she was drunk, she could have fallen down somewhere, or gotten hit by a car. Possibly she's in a hospital somewhere and we don't even know it?"

"The police have checked the hospitals out already," Wayne answered. "It's one of the first things we do."

"Or if she's not in a hospital, she could be laying somewhere on a street?"

"Unlikely," Wayne responded. "Someone would have found her and reported it. Listen, most missing person cases go cold sooner or later. People disappear and we never know why. We beg for leads, follow them, and then all of a sudden they all trickle away. We're left with nothing. It's awful for us and hell for the family, too."

Wayne started to get out of the car and Olivia stopped him. "Wait a minute," she said. "What was it like speaking to Raine's mom? What did you learn from her?"

Wayne took a second to think it over. "I learned that Raine has a totally self-absorbed mom. She keeps hatching all kinds of plots, dreaming up ideas about where her daughter might be or what happened to her. She even told me she thought you were in danger being here, and I should make you go home."

"How does she know I'm here?" Olivia was startled to hear that.

"Sean told her about you. It upset her greatly. No one has any idea why."

A moment of hopelessness swept over Olivia. She wondered if Raine had said anything about her to her mother. "I'm so sorry to hear that," she whispered.

"With a mother like that, I can see why Raine had trouble being a mom," Wayne mused. "Okay, come on, let's get into the casino. There are people there waiting to speak to us."

*

The casino was surprisingly crowded for the time of day. People were at tables, at slot machines playing blackjack, or generally drifting around. A few restaurants were open too, serving early. Music was playing and Olivia could see how Raine would thrive on the general sense of excitement wherever you went. Olivia looked more closely, though, and also saw the deep hopelessness etched on many faces as well.

"This place is a mixed bag for sure," Wayne said, as if reading Olivia's mind.

"Definitely," Olivia replied. "Okay, who do I talk to now?"

"I'll introduce you to someone in charge and then you can meet some of the people Raine saw here on a regular basis," Wayne said. "Then I have to go to the back and speak to some others who handle the money."

Olivia was very grateful for both Wayne's intelligence and his support.

"This is Andie." Wayne brought Olivia over to a short man with beady eyes and heavy jowls. "Andie, this is Olivia Wells, she's helping me out."

"Beautiful lady." Andie broke into a smile. "You always have good taste, Wayne, no doubt about it."

Wayne laughed. "Olivia's helping me find out what happened to Raine," he added.

Andie looked glum for a minute and shook his head.

"I'm going to let you talk to Olivia and I'm going in the back to talk to Pedros," Wayne continued. "You tell Olivia all she needs to know."

"I'll do that." Andie seemed pleased with the assignment. "I'll do more than that, even. I have a video of Raine. I'll show it to Olivia now."

"Great," said Wayne, "and also let her talk to some people who Raine was friends with."

"I'm on it." Andie made a fist. "Now you go see Pedros fast. He doesn't like to be kept waiting."

Wayne turned and left for the back, while Andie took Olivia's arm and shepherded her through the crowds to a medium-sized table at the other side of the casino.

"This is where Raine likes to play," Andie started. "She usually sits right here at this seat and has a ball."

"She was here the night before she left for the party?" Olivia checked one more time.

"Yes, she was," Andie agreed. "And, thankfully, we have a record of it on video."

"You video everybody?" Olivia was curious.

"There's general cameras around, of course," Andie replied. "But we zero in only when things start to get out of control. All kinds of things happen to people here and it's not our fault. We have to prove that. You come into the casino at your own risk. You're on your own."

"Raine came here often?" Olivia wanted to keep Andie talking.

"More and more the last month or so," he said. "Things were heating up."

"What things? What was happening?"

"She was going at it hard, on a roll," Andie said.

"A winning roll?" asked Olivia, alerted.

"No, she was losing her shirt," he replied. "That's the kind of roll that drives people crazy. They become determined to stop it. Come back again and again to turn it around."

"Why didn't you stop her?" Olivia knew it was an odd question, but she had to ask it anyhow. "Why didn't you call her husband?"

"Hey, hold on a minute." Andie put his hand out toward Olivia. "A person's life is private. They do what they do. We're not here as watchdogs over anyone."

Olivia bit her lips. She couldn't push too hard or offend Andie. She had to get him to show her the video.

"I understand," Olivia replied. "Can you show me the video of Raine?"

"Sure," he replied. "First you look at the video, then you can talk to her friends here if you want to."

"How well did these friends know her?" Olivia asked in a flash.

"Who knows?" Andie's voice grew rougher. "They just all play together, egg each other on. I doubt they meet each other outside."

79

"Is there anyone in particular Raine was close to?" asked Olivia.

"Nah, a few gals and a bunch of guys came to the same table night after night," Andie continued. "Come here, sit down. I'll show you the video."

Andie took Olivia a few tables away, behind a portable screen. Then he flipped open a computer and on came a video of Raine. Olivia shivered at the sight of her friend again. She was dressed in a skimpy black dress, her hair wild over her face, drunk and high at the table. Olivia watched Raine laughing wildly at nothing at all and then banging her fists on the counter uncontrollably.

"What was happening? Why was she like this?" Olivia was horrified.

"It happens," Andie said. "And it got worse and worse as the night went on. The more she lost, the wilder she acted. We finally did stop it, though. We kicked her out before she could lose more."

"Thank goodness for that," breathed Olivia. "How did she take it?"

Andie shrugged. "She didn't like it, of course, but she was too drunk to realize. One of her pals, a guy named Victor, put her into a cab and gave the driver the address to take her home."

"Home? In that condition?" asked Olivia, horrified. "What did her husband do when she returned?"

"I heard the hubby wasn't there that night," Andie grumbled. "But how do I know? I never met him. Guys like him don't come traipsing in here."

"But this happened to her a lot. He must have known," Olivia insisted.

Andie shrugged again. "I heard the hubby was always out at one meeting or another. People have a way of keeping their eyes closed when someone in the family is going downhill! It's an old story."

Olivia couldn't imagine that Sean hadn't been aware of what was happening to Raine. Why hadn't he stopped it? Or someone?

At that moment, Wayne returned, slipping into the seat beside Olivia.

"Back so quick?" Andie was surprised. "Pedros was helpful?"

"Pedros is good but I need to see Dupris," Wayne responded. "He left town suddenly yesterday, I just found out."

"No kidding!" Andie was surprised.

"Where'd be go?" asked Wayne, disturbed.

"Your guess is as good as mine," Andie shot back.

"That's not an answer!" Wayne grew insistent. "It's not possible that nobody knows where he went. I need to see Dupris!"

"So pull up a chair and hang out," Andie answered. "It's still early. Someone could come along as the night goes on and tell you where he's gone."

Wayne pulled up a chair and decided to do just that. "I'm staying here awhile," he said to Olivia. "How about you?"

Olivia had seen enough here for now. She remembered Sloane telling her to go see Miranda and she wanted to do that right now.

"I'm going to go before it gets much later, and go see Miranda," Olivia said. "I have a feeling it's important. Both Abby and Sloane suggested it."

"Good idea, you go," said Wayne. "I'm staying put where I am here now for a while."

CHAPTER FIFTEEN

Olivia put a quick call in to Miranda before she actually drove to her home. Miranda picked up, sounding blindsided, definitely not thrilled to hear from Olivia.

"I'm in the neighborhood. Can I drop by for just a few minutes?" Olivia asked.

"It's a little late to call, isn't it?" Miranda said. "I'm a busy person, I have appointments. I deserve some advance notice, don't I?"

"This won't take long." Olivia felt even more eager to see her now.

"How long exactly?" asked Miranda.

"Not long at all. Why? You're going somewhere?" Olivia asked.

"Actually, I am," Miranda quipped. "If you get here fast, I can give you fifteen minutes. No more, no less."

"Fifteen minutes is great," said Olivia. "I'll be right over, wait for me."

*

Raine quickly drove to the upscale town house community where Miranda lived, a few blocks from Raine's home. The development was safely tucked away behind a large fence with guards at the entrance, checking who was going in and out.

Olivia gave the guard her name. He checked and then buzzed her in through the electric gates. It was good that she had called first. Olivia felt she had to see Miranda, even for a few minutes.

The moment she arrived at Miranda's town house, the door flew open. "Come in," Miranda exclaimed. "What can I do for you?"

Miranda was thin and lanky with dark, wavy hair and a determined face. She was dressed for the evening, in a short, black silk dress that fit perfectly and high-heeled, open shoes. Seemed like she had a hot date for the evening.

"Sorry to come here with so little notice," Olivia started. "Looks like you have important plans."

Miranda smirked. "I don't know how important they are, but it's good to get out! I need it."

Olivia could completely understand that.

"I'm recently divorced," Miranda went on, "and I work at home alone."

Olivia was interested. "What do you do?"

"Run an online business that's gotten more successful than I ever thought and it's eating all my time up." Despite herself Miranda seemed to like Olivia.

"I'm grateful for even a few minutes," Olivia said.

Miranda stopped and looked at Olivia intently. "Okay, what can I do about this horrible mess?" she asked bitterly. "I'm just as devastated as anyone else but I refuse to sit home and cry about it. It won't do anyone any good, will it?"

Olivia found Miranda strangely impressive. There was little time now, though, and Olivia decided to jump right in.

"I heard you were the last one to see Raine alive before she disappeared," Olivia started boldly.

Miranda blanched. "Alive? Are there people saying Raine's not still alive?"

"No, I didn't mean that," said Olivia. "I just meant you were the last one to see her."

That's right, I saw her the next morning, after the party. We both went down to get breakfast at the hotel. She was fine. Everything was normal, all was well with the world."

"Raine was up early to have breakfast?" asked Olivia. "Wasn't she incredibly hungover from the night before? I would have thought she'd spend part of the day sleeping it off."

"Raine wasn't like that," Miranda interrupted. "She drank all the time and was able to hold her liquor. Yes, she was a little hungover maybe, but that was no big deal."

"What was her mood? Was she sad or depressed?" Olivia went right to the heart of it.

"Why should she be?" Miranda looked startled by the idea. "She was same as always, talking to me like she might any other morning. Depressed? Why? Raine has everything any woman could have wanted. A picture-book life and a great husband who worships the ground she walks on! Lots of the girls are secretly jealous of her, if you asked me."

"Who?" asked Olivia abruptly, wondering if Miranda was one of them.

Miranda obviously decided to let it rip then. "How about Sloane for starters? Sloane's from a poor background and has lived her life clawing her way to the top. She wasn't so thrilled with the guy she was marrying, either, and everyone knows it. Their relationship has dragged on a long time. Sloane's always hanging around Raine, looking at the life she has, comparing it to hers."

That was not the impression Olivia had of Sloane. But she'd only seen her briefly a few times.

"Who else was jealous of her?" asked Olivia, running through them all in her mind. "Nessa?"

"Why do you mention Nessa in particular?" Miranda's eyes widened.

"Nessa has a different lifestyle," said Olivia, thinking of her down in Key West with her scuba diving school.

Miranda shook her head. "I don't think Nessa's jealous of anyone. She doesn't have to be, she's too happy with her own life. In fact, some of us think Raine likes Nessa most of us all. Raine goes on lots of deepwater dives with her. In a way they are two of a kind."

"In what way?" asked Olivia, fascinated.

"They both need lots of space and do what they want when they want to, when they want it. Neither of them can stand being confined."

There were clear contradictions here and Olivia had to address them.

"I've heard that Raine is a pillar of the community, though," Olivia exclaimed.

"Not Raine, her husband, Sean," Miranda corrected her. "He's the one everybody counts on. He has to look good. But he's also the biggest stuffed shirt around. Raine does whatever he wants her to, up to a point."

"What point?" asked Olivia.

"I always wondered that myself," Miranda laughed.

What Miranda was saying made sense to Olivia. It could explain the secret and separate life Raine seemed to have. Time was running out and Olivia had to get all her questions in.

"Was Raine at all emotionally upset that morning after the party?" Olivia asked again.

"Not at all, absolutely not," Miranda insisted. "Why do you keep asking? She was talking to me about her flight home in the most casual way."

"She was looking forward to going home?"

"I wouldn't say that exactly." Miranda thought about it. "She was just planning to go back home as usual and that was that."

"What happened to her?" Olivia began to feel agitated. "What happened between the time you saw her and her trip to the airport?"

Miranda slowed down, ran her hands over her bare arms, and thought hard.

"I think she was abducted," Miranda finally breathed. "Someone nabbed her. Someone was probably watching her at casinos, could have had their eye on her a long time. She threw money around there, big time. They probably wanted some."

It made sense to Olivia.

"Or, someone at the bachelorette party spotted her. Raine drew attention to herself, was acting wild," Miranda went on.

"You mean acting wild with Luigi?" Olivia jumped on it immediately.

"Yes, that's right. You know about him?" Miranda purred.

"It's common knowledge, isn't it?" Olivia repeated.

"Sure, except not with Sean," Miranda warned. "Listen, it's possible someone will surface and ask for ransom. Or maybe it was Dupris?"

Olivia felt chilled at the mention of his name. "Why Dupris?"

"Everyone knows Raine owed Dupris fistfuls of money. I heard it never bothered him much, though. In fact, people even said Dupris liked Raine! If you know what I mean."

"Raine and Dupris were an item?" Olivia was thunderstruck.

"Can't say for sure." Miranda smirked. "But why not look a little harder? Could be Raine and Dupris are somewhere together right now?"

Just as quickly as she started talking, Miranda suddenly closed up. "Look, this is enough! I'm late. I've got to go now. There's nothing I can do about this mess anyway, is there? No point in sitting home."

Like a mini tornado then, Miranda swept out the door of her expensive town house and Olivia followed close behind.

"Let me know what happens and how it's going." Miranda waved at Olivia with the back of her hand as she jumped into a cab then and took off into the night.

As Olivia stood there watching Miranda's cab drive away, her phone rang. To her delight, it was Wayne.

"If you're free now, this would be a good time get together and debrief," Wayne said.

"Perfect timing," said Olivia. "Couldn't be better, in fact."

*

Olivia met up with Wayne in a restaurant in Coconut Grove that had soft jazz playing and a low-key atmosphere.

"I ordered a light bite for you," said Wayne, as Olivia pulled into a seat opposite him at a window table. "Cheese quiche."

Olivia smiled. "How did you know cheese quiche is my favorite?"

Wayne tapped his fingers on the table. "When you're a detective nothing escapes you. You sense all kind of little things."

Olivia was enjoying being with Wayne. She hadn't seen this playful side of him before. "Knowing that quiche is my favorite isn't so little," she said.

They both laughed. Olivia looked far out the window for a moment. The street the restaurant was on was festive, with lights on all around. It could be easy to forget what they were here for. But Wayne quickly changed the topic of conversation.

I hope your time with Miranda was valuable," he said.

"Yes, it was," Olivia answered. "Did you find anyone who could tell you where Dupris went?"

"No, I didn't." Wayne looked disgruntled. "And someone there knows. They're keeping it under the vest. I don't like it. It raises suspicions."

"When I spoke to Miranda, Dupris came up," Olivia filled Wayne in immediately.

"Really, how come?" Wayne was interested.

"Miranda said that Raine regularly owed Dupris fistfuls of money, and that he didn't seem to mind."

Wayne bristled. "Yes, but who paid this money back to him?"

"That I don't know," said Olivia.

"I'm wracking my brains about that one," Wayne added. "There are questions about Sean, too. How was it he didn't know what was going on? Raine had her separate accounts, of course, but still?"

It was a good question. Olivia had also wondered how much Sean actually knew about Raine's life. Right now it seemed he'd woken up. He was fully engaged, organizing the vigil, plastering Raine's poster everywhere, coordinating local searches, and keeping up volunteers' spirits. He was also making appearances on radio and TV, begging people to look for Raine. And begging Raine to come home. Beyond that, Sean was letting the police and Olivia take care of business.

"I know you've spoken to Sean several times," said Olivia. "What has he told you?"

"He keeps claiming everything was wonderful between them," Wayne said. "Raine had her own bank account which she wanted to keep separate from him and he respected that. Even though he's doing all the right things, he still seems to be in a daze to me. I haven't wanted to hit him with the hard facts yet. Frankly, I don't think he could take it."

Olivia felt protective of Sean as well. When she'd tried to call and speak to him, she'd also had the impression he was still in a daze, couldn't listen to anything.

"There may be a good reason why Sean's in a daze," Olivia added. "There's lots of stuff he could be blocking! Miranda also mentioned to me that she thought Dupris liked Olivia."

"Liked her? In what way?" Wayne looked startled.

"Miranda wondered if Olivia and Dupris weren't somewhere together right now?" Olivia added, hesitantly.

"What? This is huge." Wayne was all over it. "You think Raine's been cheating on Sean left and right?"

"I didn't say that," said Olivia.

"But it's possible, isn't it? You can't deny it." Wayne seemed stung by the suggestion. "I'll get investigators looking into it immediately. Is that how Raine was getting her debt paid? Sleeping with Dupris?"

"Hold on." Olivia was upset. "I wasn't suggesting that."

"But Miranda was," said Wayne.

Olivia wanted to backtrack fast. "I wouldn't put that much stock in Miranda's observations. She seems edgy and nervous, like someone who would say whatever came into her mind. Miranda also cast suspicion on Sloane."

"Sloane? Which one is that?" Wayne was listening intently.

"Sloane's the bride-to-be," said Olivia. "I met her briefly twice and had a completely different impression of her than what Miranda said."

"These girls are good at hiding," Wayne spoke slowly. "You see one thing about them one minute and something very different the next. Look at Raine, for example."

"You're referring to her fling with the stripper?" Olivia asked, wondering if Wayne was holding that against her.

"That's just the tip of the iceberg," Wayne replied. "A gambling addiction like the one Raine has is serious. It opens you to all kinds of trouble, including blackmail, drugs, you name it."

Olivia suddenly felt deeply sad for Raine, wondering how she'd fallen so far down this slippery slope.

"Gambling addictions affect the entire family," Wayne continued. "I know firsthand. My brother Len had a rotten gambling addiction. It drove my dad nuts, consumed him."

"That's awful," said Olivia, fascinated to learn more about Wayne's personal life. "What finally happened to your brother?"

"It took a long, long time, but my dad finally got him into serious rehab. Len's clean of it now." Wayne smiled. "In fact, he just got married to a terrific gal."

"Congratulations," said Olivia.

"Thanks." Wayne smiled as the delicious, steaming quiches arrived for both of them. "I have three brothers who are all married now. I'm the only bachelor left in the family. People are beginning to give up on me, too. Everyone tells me I'm a lost cause."

Olivia laughed as she bit into the quiche. "Well, you've got plenty of company who are lost causes," she replied. "In fact, you're looking at one."

Wayne smiled back. "Lost causes or not, we're doing good work. And, next step is that I'm getting ready to have all the women down to Key West to be officially interviewed at the station."

"Great," Olivia jumped in. "I just want to speak to Sloane alone first before they all get together."

"Fine with me," said Wayne. "Let me know when you're ready and I'll call them all down there."

Olivia and Wayne looked at each other silently. "It's good working with you." Wayne was the first to break the strange silence.

"Good working with you, too," said Olivia. "Do you think we've got a shot?"

"A shot at what?" Wayne looked startled.

"At finding Raine alive and well?" Olivia replied.

"All bets are off right now," Wayne replied quietly. "Time is passing   and   nothing   is   solid   yet."

CHAPTER SIXTEEN

As Olivia expected, Sloane was still at Raine's house the next morning when she called. Sloane picked up the phone immediately.

"I need time to talk to you as soon as possible." Olivia wasn't mincing words and Sloane sensed the urgency.

"Why? Something's happened? You have new developments?" Sloane's voice got shrill.

"Every minute that passes there are new developments," said Olivia, "though we're not aware of what they all may be."

"Okay, I get it. Time's running out." Sloane calmed down. "Come over in an hour. I'll be ready then."

*

When Sloane opened the door and Olivia walked into Raine's house, it was unnaturally quiet and dark. The sense of gloom had definitely deepened. Sloane reflected it too, standing there dressed in loose slacks and a tight shirt with her hair messy.

"Rough night?" Olivia asked.

"Rough night, rough morning, rough everything." Sloane ran her hands through her hair. "Hope is dwindling here. Raine's mom's going nuts, her boyfriend is here and Raine's father refuses to come over."

"Doesn't sound pleasant," Olivia commented.

"That's an understatement if I ever heard one." Sloane rubbed her hand over her face. "I'm now basically the one taking full care of Clea."

"At least you're a stable, solid presence around," Olivia added.

"I don't know how stable I am, but I'm here," Sloane murmured.

"Is your fiancé around too?" asked Olivia.

"He's been here once or twice for a few minutes." Sloane looked at Olivia strangely. "It's not like him to be overly concerned about anything. He takes it as it comes. Always has, always will."

"Overly concerned? This is a life-and-death situation!" Olivia was startled.

"I know, but that's how he is." Sloane shrugged. "By now I've accepted everything about him."

Olivia wondered if indeed that was true. How could Sloane accept her fiancé being absent at a time like this?

"Listen, we're not here to talk about my fiancé." Sloane obviously wanted to change the topic. "Let's go into the side den and talk. We'd be better off not going into the main room. We don't want Raine's mom to run into you. She's half off her rocker by now. She'll talk a blue streak about nothing. She thinks they're all out to get each one of us, keeps wondering who's next."

"How about Sean?" Olivia asked, wondering how he was surviving this. "I haven't seen him for a while."

"He's out now," Sloane said abruptly. "His search teams are moving into two more counties and Sean's in charge of it."

"How's he handling things?" Olivia asked.

"Hanging in," said Sloane, as she started walking to the side den. "Sean's still convinced Raine's alive. So, I guess that's helping him get through the days. After everything, he's still in love with her."

Olivia sensed the pain that caused Sloane. "And you?" she asked as they walked into the small, dark den, filled with books, old family photos, and two small sofas.

"I have no idea if she's alive or dead," Sloane said. "I mean this was supposed to be the most joyful time of my life, wasn't it? And Raine's ruined it. It's all about her now. But it always was. She never knew how good she had it. Always wanted more and better. Looking for her next high."

Olivia could see how tired Sloane was as she rambled on.

"I've had enough. I have to say something now," Sloane burst out. "Raine's got the greatest guy that anyone could want, and how does she handle it? She runs to Key West all the time! And not just to gamble!"

Olivia began to get chills running up and down her arm. "What did Raine go there for? You have to tell me."

Sloane stood up and walked threateningly to Olivia. "Listen," she said in a hoarse tone. "Olivia went down to Key West regularly because she has someone there. Not just a stripper, or one-night stand. She has a real lover on the side. I even know who he is and where he hangs out. I also happen to know that the two of them had a huge fight right before the bachelorette party. That same night."

"How do you know all this?" Olivia jumped up.

"I can't tell you how I know everything," Sloane whispered, "but I even heard both of them yelling at each other that night. Raine was giving him an ultimatum of some sort. He's not the kind of guy who does well with that."

"You have to tell me how you know this!" Olivia insisted.

"No, I don't, I don't have to do anything. I'm giving you this information out of the goodness of my heart, but I don't have to tell you anything else." Sloane wouldn't budge an inch.

"Does Sean know about this? Did you tell him?" Olivia insisted.

"In my way I tried to suggest it a few times." Sloane's eyes were flashing. "But he's too stupid to catch on. And he won't listen. He can't. If he listened to a word of what I said, his whole world would come crumbling down. He would have to make all kinds of changes. So he listens to what suits him. And no more."

Like all of us, thought Olivia. "Why did you even try to tell him?" Olivia was curious.

"Because he's a good man and he doesn't deserve this!" Sloane began to grow angry. "He deserves someone who cares about him! Not someone who constantly disses him behind his back!"

Olivia looked at Sloane with great intensity. "He deserves someone like you?" Olivia asked sharply.

Sloane swayed a moment and then regained her footing. "Sure, why not? Someone like me!" she answered boldly. "Someone who's here for him in times of trouble! Is there something wrong with that?"

"Nothing wrong except he's married to Raine!" Olivia answered unsparingly.

"This is not a marriage," Sloane shot back fiercely. "It's a horse-and-pony show. They look great together, have a gorgeous house and beautiful baby. But Raine runs away regularly and then returns. Sean keeps it quiet. He made all kinds of excuses to himself. But maybe this time she ran too far, for too long. Maybe she even forgot the way home?"

Olivia took a painful, craggy breath. Had Raine just run away again for longer than usual, without telling anyone? Even though Sloane was personally involved, she was smart. It was clear, though, that Sloane couldn't stand Raine and wanted Sean for herself.

"Did you hope Sean would find out about Raine one day, and turn to you?" Olivia asked Sloane then.

"You're bright, you're sharp, but it doesn't matter what I hoped," Sloane replied. "You get what you get in life. I was ready to finally get married. I was even looking forward to it, and then Raine went missing!" Sloane's eyes filled with tears.

"Will you give me the contact information for Raine's lover and exactly where I can find him?" Olivia asked.

"Yes, I will." Sloane seemed suddenly delighted by the thought of it. "His name is Victor. I'll get you the name and address of the club he hangs out in down in Key West. Go talk to him and you'll find everything I said is true."

"I don't disbelieve you," Olivia answered.

"But you don't like me, either." Sloane flung her head back. "You probably think I have ulterior motives for being here with Sean now."

"You said that, I didn't," Olivia replied.

Sloane laughed at that. "How'd you get so smart? You're not a real detective, are you? I heard you've just started doing this after your own fiancé was killed."

The sudden memory of Todd felt like a cold knife thrust at Olivia. It stung.

"That's right," Olivia realized, "I've just started doing this work, but everything in my life has prepared me for it."

Sloane walked closer. "And everything in my life has prepared me also, for staying here with Sean. If life suddenly presents a U-turn in the road, I'm not going to keep walking past it, am I?"

Olivia wondered where that U-turn was going to lead, and if they'd ever find Raine on it.

"I need the contact information for Victor, now," Olivia said to Sloane, crisply.

Sloane gave Olivia the club Victor could be found at in Key West, and a crumpled photo of him. Victor was a tall, surprisingly surly-looking guy in his late thirties with thick black hair, an uneasy smile, and a long tattoo on his right arm. Olivia shuddered. She couldn't imagine that he would be someone Raine would be drawn to.

"He's tough, but he's fun," Sloane commented. "Raine said she feels like herself with him, doesn't have to pretend to be someone she's not."

"Did you ever ask Raine to tell Sean about him?" asked Olivia.

"I did," Sloane replied, "but, of course, she wouldn't. Raine said what Sean didn't know wouldn't hurt him. It was all a day's fun."

*

After Sloane left the den to care for the baby, Olivia stayed a few moments more. She wanted to check Raine's Facebook page to see if any photos of Victor appeared anywhere. She also had to give this information to Wayne immediately, so they could check

Raine's cell phone records and other social media to see if anything from Victor appeared.

As Olivia sat scrolling through the Facebook pages, Raine's entire life rolled out in front of her eyes. Beautiful friends, wonderful photographs that Raine had taken and was selling. There were also photos of her and Sean at charity balls, along with a few pictures of Raine holding her daughter, as if she were the best mom in the world. Nowhere at all did Olivia see a glimpse of Victor haunting the pages. In a sense that was to be expected. Raine's presentation to the world was streamlined and edited for the perfect audience. But the darker truth of her life, which was bubbling up to the surface to be seen now, had stayed carefully hidden for years.

Olivia closed the computer quickly and sat there in the dark room. She would go back down to Key West soon to talk to Victor. Wayne would also be calling the girls to come down soon. Other than that, where was the case going? Was Victor the missing link? Olivia felt uneasy, as if there were something else she was missing; something that was there right in front of her eyes. What was it? She was both uncertain and sure of it at the same time.

CHAPTER SEVENTEEN

Olivia immediately called Wayne and told him about Victor. To her surprise, Wayne took it in stride, though. It didn't seem to surprise or bother him as much as it did Olivia.

"We see this all the time," Wayne said flatly. "Wives cheat, husbands cheat. It's a tough world out there. A solid marriage these days is as rare as a shooting star. Maybe you can count them on the finger of one hand."

Olivia felt saddened both by Wayne's words and by Raine's behavior as well. Was that why Wayne hadn't ever married? It seemed like he'd grown bitter, seeing too much of the dark side of life.

"It's a good idea for you to come back to Key West, though, and talk to the lover," Wayne agreed. "I'm headed down there as well. Why don't we take the next flight down together?"

Olivia liked the idea. She called Sean to let him know she'd be leaving Miami shortly.

"You're doing a phenomenal job, Olivia," Sean replied. "I'll always be grateful to you for it."

Olivia wondered exactly what Sean was referring to, and how he even knew what she'd been doing. They'd hardly been in touch.

"Thanks," she said. "I'm definitely trying."

"That's all we can do is try," Sean staunchly replied. "The rest is out of our hands. It's in God's hands. Our entire church is praying for Raine constantly."

Olivia was glad that gave Sean comfort, but the nervousness in his voice belied his calm words.

"Keep in touch with me from Key West," Sean said then. "It's good you're going back down there."

"Why?" asked Olivia.

"Because that's where Raine was when she disappeared. That's where she went frequently. If she's hiding out somewhere, you'll find her there."

"Where could she be hiding, Sean?" Olivia asked immediately.

Sean suddenly laughed strangely. "If I knew I'd be there in an instant myself, swoop her up and carry her back to our home, no matter how much she kicked and screamed."

"Why would she kick and scream?" Sean's words jarred Olivia. "Wouldn't she be grateful to be found and taken home?"

"I would hope so, I really would." Sean's voice constricted.

94

"You would hope so, but you're not sure?" Olivia quickly asked.

"I didn't say that." Sean was quick on the trigger. "I said I would really hope she'd be grateful. In fact, I'm sure she would."

After the conversation, Olivia hung up feeling both sad and odd.

*

The plane ride down to Key West was quick and easy and neither Wayne nor Olivia spoke much at first. As the plane lifted off, Olivia felt a wave of exhaustion. Time and hope were definitely running out. She even began to feel as though at this point it was possible that they were just going through the motions of finding her friend. There was nothing definite as yet to hold onto.

Wayne seemed to be having the opposite reaction. "I was just thinking, maybe we should slow down and turn down the heat on the case a bit," he suggested. "We have no direct evidence that anything has happened. And, given Raine's impulsive nature, right now it's entirely possible she's run off with someone of her own free will."

Olivia wondered who he was thinking of. "Dupris?" she asked.

Wayne raised his eyebrows. "Him or a host of other characters in her life. The important thing to remember is that there have been no calls for ransom, no physical evidence or body found."

"Thankfully," breathed Olivia, wondering why Wayne was having this change of heart. Was it because he heard that Raine had a lover, Victor?

"As I said," Wayne continued, "there's no evidence that Raine just didn't just ditch her life and go somewhere to start over. You'd be surprised how often it happens. Especially when there's a lover in the picture."

"I would be surprised," Olivia replied.

"You keep finding out things about people you could never imagine when you do this work," Wayne remarked. "You'll see for yourself."

"Right now I'm feeling that I know much more than I want to," Olivia replied as the plane took a quick dip, flinging them together.

Olivia pulled back quickly and so did Wayne.

"Give it a chance," Wayne remarked. "You've been thrown into a hotbed. First losing your fiancé and then looking for a missing friend! It's not usually so personal."

How it could not be? "Is it good to detach yourself, though?" she asked. "Become cold and heartless?"

"It's not detaching yourself, it's being professional." Wayne took exception. "It's a skill you acquire. Lorna does it beautifully. She constantly accuses me of caring too much, not being professional. In fact, it gets on her nerves tremendously."

Olivia hadn't thought of Lorna for quite some time and the sound of her name jarred her.

"Is Lorna still on the case? I haven't heard a word about her for a while."

"Barely," said Wayne. "The department has lots of other things for her to take on."

Olivia caught the upset in his voice. "Are you guys having a hard time working together?" she asked lightly.

"Very," Wayne answered. "You nailed it. It's really rough going right now."

It crossed Olivia's mind briefly how odd it was that fate had brought her to Wayne's side at this moment, to work with him on this case. He was getting a taste of something different. Olivia hoped that in the future Wayne could find a work partner better suited to him. He certainly deserved it.

*

The plane had an easy landing and they caught a cab and got back into Key West in no time. As soon as Olivia was settled back at her hotel, she lay down on the couch and looked out the window. A sense of deep loneliness swept over her. Had she herself done what Wayne thought about Raine? Had Olivia ditched her life to run away to start another? It was a startling thought and she had to give it consideration. Was being a detective a life Olivia wanted for herself? Could she tolerate it even? What kind of future could it bring? After Olivia found out about Todd, she thought she never wanted another relationship. But, lying here on the couch alone now, she began to wonder. It would certainly be good to have someone to share all this with for the long term. In fact, right now, it seemed essential.

*

The club Victor frequented was located under a cluster of old gnarled trees on a back road in Key West, in a less than safe neighborhood. Olivia decided to dress for the occasion, so she would fit in and not raise any questions. She slipped into a silky, blue, fitted dress and brushed her long, blonde hair until it shone. Then she threw a shiny top over her shoulders and left, just as if she were simply going out for an evening of fun.

The club wasn't hard to find. When Olivia arrived, it was rocking with music. Olivia made her way to the front door and entered easily. The place was packed, smoky and noisy, with people clustered close to each other, talking nonstop.

Olivia went to the bar and immediately asked whether Victor was here. The bartender, a big, jovial guy, threw back his head and laughed.

"Victor's always here. Go to the room in back. There's another bar there. He'll be hanging at it."

"Thanks," said Olivia. Acting as though there wasn't another place in the world she'd rather be, she made her way through the crowds to the back.

The back room was a little less crowded, but equally smoky and noisy. Once again Olivia went to the bar and was about to ask for Victor, when she saw a tall guy, who looked just like his photo, standing almost next to her. Olivia scrutinized him carefully in the dim light. He matched the photo exactly, with the long tattoo on his arm. In person he was even more good-looking, though. The only difference was the slightly threatening air he had about him, which Olivia hadn't picked up on.

Olivia walked over to him, smiling, "Victor?" she asked.

Victor snapped to attention and looked at Olivia, scanning her from head to toe.

"Yeah?" he asked, not impressed. Clearly, she wasn't his type.

"I'm a close friend of Raine's," Olivia said immediately.

At that Victor narrowed his eyes. "She sent you to see me?" he asked, irritated.

"I only wish she had," Olivia replied. "Raine's still missing. You've heard about it, I'm sure."

"Of course I heard!" he retorted. "I heard everything. What do you think I am, some kind of jerk?"

Olivia backed off. This guy seemed like a living time bomb. She couldn't find anything redeeming about him at all. Olivia would have to go slow questioning him.

"Of course I don't think you're a jerk," she quipped. "I know that you and Raine had a close relationship, and I just wanted to talk to you a bit."

That didn't sit well with Victor, either. "I wouldn't exactly call it a close relationship." He rubbed one hand along his arm. "We knew each other. We hung out."

It definitely sounded like Victor was covering for something, thought Olivia.

"I saw Raine here at the club when she was in Key West," Victor continued. "I live here, have a house near the swamp."

"Do you work down here, too?" Olivia asked, wondering if he was some kind of drifter who lived off the women he found.

"I certainly do," he answered. "Have a woodworking shop in my house. I build cabinets, do repairs. People hire me regularly. Anything else you want to know?" His voice took on a threatening tone now.

"We're all very worried about Raine," Olivia responded, trying to redirect the conversation.

"There's no point in it!" Victor burst out. "I'm not worried in the least. This is vintage Raine. She's around somewhere, playing a game. Raine loves to play games of all kinds. She's just upping the ante now."

Olivia only wished it were so, but standing here in this swarmy club beside Victor, she began to fear otherwise. What in the world had Raine seen in this guy? What was it that attracted her to him?

"I heard you and Raine had a fight right before the bachelorette party." Olivia had to prod him to say more.

To her surprise, Victor grinned. "We had a fight like usual, not good or bad. It's the way things were. She expected too much. I got tired of it."

"What did she expect?" Olivia felt agitated. For all she knew this was the heart of the matter. This fight could have been the beginning of her disappearance.

"Raine expected everything of everyone else," Victor surprisingly answered. "But what would she give you back in return? Not much, really! I told her in the beginning what she could expect from me! She wouldn't take it, kept pushing the edges. I hate it like hell when women push the edges. Make you feel like crap for no reason at all."

Olivia felt disturbed talking to him. "Where do you think she is now?" she asked on a long shot.

"I have no idea and couldn't care less." Victor tried to shrug Olivia off.

Olivia wouldn't have it. "Wait a minute, I have another question."

"Yeah, and why should I answer? Who the hell are you anyway?"

"I'm a detective, working the case," Olivia answered boldly. It was the first time she'd identified herself as a detective and it felt powerful to do so.

"A detective?" Victor's eyes opened wide. "You actually tracked me down here? Why? I already refused to talk to the police about this. There's no reason I should. They have nothing on me."

Olivia wasn't aware of that. "When did you last see or speak to Raine?" She plunged on, anyway.

"I saw her right before the party when we had that fight," Victor answered, despite himself.

"You didn't see or speak to her at all after that?" Olivia wanted to be certain.

"I said I didn't, and I don't lie." Victor's jaw clenched. "Don't pull me into this dame's life. I don't need it and don't belong there." Then he turned swiftly away. "And if you don't mind," he said over his shoulder, "the best thing you can do for me right now is get lost. I'm meeting someone else here in a few minutes."

Offended and fascinated at the same time, Olivia backed off. She carefully blended into the crowd, so he wouldn't see her. Who was Victor was about to meet? she wondered. Probably some other woman in town, out for a hot night. It was troubling that Victor was seeing someone else so soon after Raine had disappeared. And to top it off, he seemed to have no concern about what had happened to her. None of it computed with him or made the slightest difference. It was possible he'd even been seeing this other person before Raine disappeared. Was that what their fight was about? Olivia wondered. Did Raine find out about this other woman and get angry? Did Victor get rid of her to shut her up?

Olivia craned her neck through the crowd to watch what Victor was doing and who exactly he was waiting for.

In a few seconds he went to the other end of the bar, sat down at it, and ordered a drink. Their talk had obviously left him nervous and Olivia was glad to see that, at least.

In a few minutes a slim woman in high-heeled shoes came toward him. Victor quickly turned toward her and stretched out his arms. The woman looked familiar. In the dim light of the club it was hard making out who she was, though. Olivia craned her neck and looked more closely.

To Olivia's horror, she saw Miranda rush to Victor's side, fling her arms around his shoulders, and nestle up to him. Miranda and

Victor? What in the world could it mean? Olivia was totally thunderstruck.

CHAPTER EIGHTEEN

Olivia ran out of the club and put an immediate call in to Wayne.

"What does it mean that it's Miranda that Victor was meeting?" she yelled.

"Calm down, calm down," Wayne answered. "Victor's allowed to see whoever he wants. Raine's a married woman, remember?"

Wayne's even tone calmed Olivia somewhat. "Yes, that's right, I have to remember," she said. "Why haven't the cops spoken to Victor yet, though?"

"He hasn't been willing to talk." Wayne was reassuring. "But he will. It's all in the timing. You're doing great, Olivia. You're helping a lot. We have to go step by step. One piece of information builds on another."

"But what does it mean?" Olivia's heart was still beating fast. "How could Raine's close friend do something like this to her?"

"We don't know yet, Olivia," Wayne repeated. "You have to calm down. Pretty soon everything will be obvious."

"You really think so?" Olivia asked.

"Yes, I do," he said softly.

"But you said most missing person's cases grow cold." Olivia was confused. Her encounter with Victor had disturbed her more than she realized.

"Most cases do go cold," Wayne repeated. "I'm not saying we'll find Olivia for sure, but I do think we're on the edge of getting a lot more insight. Things will be revealed. I've contacted Raine's friends, and also Sean and Raine's father. They're all going to be at the station in Key West, early tomorrow. First we'll talk to each friend separately and then together in a group. Hopefully, we'll get new information."

Olivia didn't know if that was enough for her. "I don't just need new information," she shot back. "I need to find Raine and bring her home!"

"I know you do." Wayne's voice was kind and soothing. "But that I can't guarantee you. Just come to the station early tomorrow. You'll be part of everything. We're actually trying to get Victor to join us as well. My guess is he'll show up sooner or later."

Olivia was repelled by the idea of Victor being there as well. "He's awful. I don't want to ever see him again."

"He's a huge piece of the puzzle," Wayne added. "We'll be lucky to get him there. And we've got to approach him in the right way, or he'll balk!"

"Do your best," Olivia agreed.

Wayne laughed. "I always do my best, in case you hadn't noticed."

"I have noticed," Olivia replied right away. "You do a wonderful job, Wayne."

A long pause greeted Olivia on the other end of the phone. "Well, it's certainly refreshing to hear someone say that," Wayne replied.

"Of course it is, and it's true," Olivia repeated.

"Okay, get to the station tomorrow mid-morning." Wayne turned businesslike again. "Raine's friends will be pleased to see you. Once they're all together in a room, we'll put them under pressure and hope one of them will get really frazzled and let something rip."

*

The next morning Olivia had a long breakfast in her room before she left for the station. This was going to be a big day and she wanted to be ready for it. Finishing up her coffee, she couldn't help but think of both Todd and Victor. On the surface they couldn't be more different. Todd had been polished, charming, and sleek. He was smart, intelligent, successful. Victor was unruly, uncaring, and impolite. He didn't seem to care a bit about the impression he made either, or what might be expected of him. Yet, deep down, Olivia wondered if Todd and Victor weren't exactly alike. Both played around with women and thought nothing of it. Both left a stream of broken hearts in their wake. Was it because of Victor that Raine conveniently disappeared?

Olivia put her coffee cup down, dressed carefully, and headed to the police station. The police would be interviewing each one alone before they were put together as a group. It would be fascinating to see them all together, thought Olivia. Especially to watch Miranda. Was she complicit in Raine's disappearance? Olivia thought it was entirely possible now.

*

Nessa was the first to jump up off the bench when Olivia walked into the station and rush over to her.

"I'm truly happy to see you." Nessa hugged Olivia warmly. "This is hell. Where is Raine?"

Abby got up and came over to Olivia as well. "Each day that goes by is worse and worse," she breathed. "Raine's father is in the next room, pulling himself together. He's completely wrecked by now. Sean's on the way down separately. Should be here in a few minutes."

Olivia took it all in. Raine's friends were definitely on edge. Pietra sat sullenly on the bench in the corner and waved to Olivia from where she was. Olivia waved back.

"Where's Sloane?" asked Olivia, noticing her absence.

"She's been in the bathroom since they finished talking with her." Abby gave Olivia a knowing glance. "Who knows what went on there?"

"What do you mean?" asked Olivia, startled.

"Sloane's complicated," Nessa jumped in. "Always was, always will be."

"She'll be out in a second, you can ask her yourself," said Abby.

Olivia looked forward to it.

"I heard that Sean will be joining us when we all talk," Nessa said then in a hoarse whisper. "That's good. Very good. He needs to wake up."

"He's doing the best he can do," Abby interjected. "We all are. And the police know it."

At that moment Sloane walked into the room, threw a glance at Olivia, smiled, and walked to the bench, waiting for the group interrogation.

"She looks okay enough, doesn't she?" Abby whispered to Nessa then.

"Looks don't mean anything," Nessa spit back, as Sean suddenly entered, strangely collected, wearing linen pants and a navy summer blazer.

"Thank you all for being here," Sean said to no one in particular, looking around.

"There's just Miranda inside now," said Nessa. "As soon as she comes out with Wayne, we'll begin."

"Good, very good," Sean repeated, as if he were in total control.

Almost as soon as Sean finished his sentence, Wayne and Miranda walked into the room. Looking calm and completely professional, Wayne gazed at everyone.

"Okay," Wayne said, as Miranda joined the other girls on the bench. "Chief of Police Arnold Tan will be joining us in a moment, and then we'll begin. Good to see you, Sean."

Sean simply nodded.

"I believe Raine's father is expected as well," Wayne added, looking at Olivia.

"He's in the next room collecting himself," Abby piped up. "He needs some quiet first. This is a lot for him. He'll come in later."

"That's absolutely fine," Wayne replied.

Then, to the surprise of everyone, the door pushed open, and Victor entered gruffly.

There was a rustle of surprise among all the women as Wayne immediately went over to greet him.

"Thanks for joining us, Victor," Wayne commented, as Nessa threw Miranda a sideward glance. "We certainly appreciate all the help we can get."

Victor grumbled something and threw a glance at Sean, who didn't look back.

Chief of Police Arnold Tan suddenly joined them.

"Okay," said Wayne then, pointing to a long table in the room. "You'll sit around this table together, and we'll get started immediately."

Everyone in the room got up then and took a place at the table without commenting. Olivia, Wayne, and Chief Tan sat at a small table opposite them.

Chief of Police Tan opened the meeting. "As you all know," he started, "up to now we don't have anything specific. It's not looking good. We don't want the case to go cold. I'm hoping someone here can tell us something that will really help us."

Dead silence filled the room.

"We've spoken to each of you separately," Chief Tan went on. "Now that you're all together, maybe something one of you says will jog a memory in someone else."

Olivia saw Sean glancing at Victor slowly out of the corner of his eye. Olivia wondered if Sean knew who he was. Victor did not return the glance, only sat in his chair looking out the window, a resigned look on his face.

"Was there any possible warning that Raine was thinking of leaving on her own?" Wayne started the questioning.

A brittle moment of tension filled the room.

"As far as I'm concerned, she could have taken off at any moment," Nessa piped up. "Raine loved adventure. She needed it."

"Yes, she did." Pietra echoed Nessa's words. "And every one of us knew that."

"Not every single one." Miranda seemed on edge. "I saw different sides of her."

"There are different sides of everyone here." Pietra seemed upset by Miranda.

"We're all good people, though, very good," Abby insisted.

"This isn't about us," Sloane interrupted. "We're here to help find Raine, aren't we?"

Sean half stood in his seat then. "Raine might have enjoyed some adventure," he proclaimed, "but she also loved the family and our life together. She took her time away, but she always returned. She needed to return, was happy to be home. I believe she's still alive somewhere, waiting to return to us right now."

"What happened to her, Sean?" Wayne asked pointedly.

The same question over and over, thought Olivia. Each time with a different echo.

"I have no idea what happened, none at all," Sean insisted.

"I believe Raine has been abducted," Miranda suddenly burst out. She seemed to have had enough of this.

"By who? Why?" Sean's face grew red.

"Raine had big gambling debts, didn't she, Sean?" Miranda stared at him head on.

"She had some debts," Sean said finally, "and I paid them all. Every last one of them!"

The room grew silent and stiff. This was an important piece of information that Olivia had not heard before.

"In fact, I thought it was Dupris who paid them," Miranda shot forth.

Sean stood up boldly. "Dupris held the debt and I paid it," he repeated emphatically.

"Where's Dupris now?" Miranda couldn't be stopped.

"What's it to you?" Sean flung out at her.

"Dupris's out of town right now, isn't he?" she said. "We're wondering why."

"I wouldn't know," Sean interjected. "And what has that got to do with anything?"

"Sit down, Sean, and calm down, Miranda." Wayne took charge. "There's absolutely no evidence that Dupris being out of town has anything at all to do with Raine's disappearance."

"This is a witch hunt!" Nessa stood up then. "These girls know things I never even heard of. They're not Raine's true friends. Not one of them."

Abby closed her eyes. "Nessa is overly emotional all the time," she uttered. "We are Raine's very best friends. If Raine were here she would tell you that herself."

"Stop," Pietra demanded. "Raine's been gone too long. It's no good to pretend. It's only the truth that will help us find her."

"It's too late for that, too late for everything," Miranda hissed, as Victor's face grew darker.

"Why is it too late?" Olivia sprang to her feet.

"Why are we walking on tiptoe?" Miranda flung back. "We all know what happened at the party. We all know about Raine and Luigi!"

"Who the hell is Luigi?" Sean jumped up again.

"Shut up, bitch," Sloane flung at Miranda. "You're no one to talk about anything."

"Someone has to," Miranda insisted. "And I'm willing to talk about me and Victor, too."

"Who is Luigi?" Sean demanded. "What in hell are you talking about?"

"A dancer at the party," Miranda flung out, as Victor walked over to her and grabbed her shoulders.

"Enough, enough," Victor muttered.

"Sean"—Wayne took it in another direction now—"you said you paid Raine's debts for her. Did you also know Dupris?"

"I knew him in passing," Sean commented. "Who's Luigi?"

"You knew your wife had a gambling addiction?" Wayne continued.

Sean grew silent and sad. "I knew she gambled," he answered quietly then. "I wouldn't call it an addiction. Who's Luigi, another lender? Did she owe money to him?"

"No, not that I know of," Wayne answered.

Abby put her head in her hands then. "Is it absolutely necessary to pull out all the dirt hidden under the covers?" she cried out. "Don't you know lots of people are going to get hurt?"

"Lots of people are hurting right now." Sloane took Abby on. "It is necessary for everyone to know what happened. We're grown-ups, we can handle it."

"We have to handle it," Pietra echoed, "including you."

"What truth?" Sean looked as if he were going to explode.

Sloane threw Miranda a warning glance and proceeded. "Raine was having an affair with Victor," Sloane announced. "She came down to Key West regularly to sleep with him behind Sean's back."

Sean didn't bat an eyelid. He stood rigidly without moving.

"I tried to tell you that over and over, Sean," Sloane suddenly pleaded with Sean.

"Is that true, Victor?" Wayne turned to him directly.

"I'm not denying it," Victor replied. "Let's get this out and over with and move on."

Sean turned in Victor's direction. "You and Raine?" was all he could say.

"Raine never said a word to me about you, fella," Victor replied.

"Why you?" Sean couldn't seem to comprehend it.

"It didn't mean much," Victor answered roughly. "She wasn't the love of my life."

"I'm the love of Victor's life," Miranda interjected.

Police Chief Tan focused on Miranda. "You wanted Raine out of the way, didn't you then?" he asked bluntly.

"Frankly, I couldn't have cared less," said Miranda. "Raine was a married woman, playing games. Her affair with Victor was coming to an end, anyway. I'm the love of Victor's life."

"You're disgusting," Abby practically hissed at Miranda. "Raine was a good friend of yours."

"Get a life," Miranda shot back. "Good friend or not, she didn't own Victor. She had enough already, didn't she?"

"That's what I said," Sloane agreed. "Raine always had everything she ever wanted."

"Wait a minute, wait a minute." Sean seemed to be having trouble catching his breath. "Slow down. I want to hear this again. I don't believe a word of it."

"Believe it or not, it's the truth," Sloane interjected. "It's the dead truth, and I knew it all along."

"The dead truth?" murmured Nessa. "Raine died for it? Someone killed her?"

Sean suddenly collapsed on his chair as Sloane rushed over to him.

"Our marriage was perfect," Sean kept repeating as Sloane ran her hands slowly over his back.

Victor stood and looked at Sean oddly. "No marriage is perfect, fella," he muttered. "Only a jackass believes that."

Sean looked up at Victor strangely then, almost like compatriots. At that moment Olivia couldn't help wonder if Sean had seen Victor before.

"Do you know Victor? Have you seen him before?" she asked Sean bluntly.

But Sean just put his head down into his hands now and lapsed into silence.

"Sean's a good man, he doesn't deserve this," Sloane interrupted, as the door to the room suddenly flung open then and Raine's enraged father walked in.

CHAPTER NINETEEN

"Okay, enough, enough." Edward burst into the room, looking as if he were going to tear his hair out. Olivia couldn't remember ever seeing a man looking so dismayed.

"This is Raine's father," Wayne announced to Chief of Police Tan.

"He's late," Chief Tan replied.

"Not late, early," Edward snapped back. "Don't think I've been just hanging around doing nothing, either. I've hired the best private investigators in town and I've been in the next room talking to them. They're coming close to something and we'll have big news very soon. They're just double checking to be sure."

"Who asked you to hire your own investigators?" Sean exclaimed, jumping up. "This is my wife who's missing."

"What kind of news can we expect?" Chief Tan bristled.

Olivia had a moment of horror, fearing it was over, that they'd found her body.

"They haven't found a body, have they?" Olivia cried out as the entire room suddenly froze.

"I didn't say that, did I?" Edward turned to her, aghast. "I said, big news!"

"Probably another sighting," Wayne leaned over and whispered to Olivia. "He's hanging onto any hope."

"There's been absolutely no physical evidence." Chief Tan turned to Olivia as well. "We have not declared the case a homicide."

"Not yet," Edward growled.

"Sit down, please, Edward." Wayne stood up then to calm him down.

"I repeat"—Sean remained standing—"who asked you to hire a private investigator? Raine is my wife. I'm in charge."

"And she's my daughter, in case you don't happen to remember!" Edward countered intensely. "You're responsible for her and look what's happened."

"So, this is my fault now, too?" Sean was beside himself. "Whatever bad happens in Raine's life is because of me?"

"Well, isn't it?" Edward fumed. "What's happened good to her since you've married?"

"You refuse to see anything good," Sean countered. "You love trouble, don't you?"

"I love trouble?" Edward was appalled. "You did all you could to turn Raine against me. I was a fabulous father all the years, though. Gave her everything she needed."

Sean wouldn't go along with that for a second. "Raine's father made life hell on earth for us," he said to no one in particular. "From the minute we married he practically disowned her. Whatever she wanted from him, the answer was no."

"That's absolutely right," Edward agreed. "Once you married her she belonged to you! But you still expected me to take care of everything."

Sean threw back his head. "A father loves his daughter always, he takes care of her."

Edward smiled slowly and chillingly and turned directly to the Chief of Police. "Raine started to really go downhill after she married Sean," he went on. "Everything about this marriage was awful for her. She began drinking and drugging more and more. Anyone could see that."

"It's not true." Sloane stood up fiercely, shaking her head. "Sean was good to Raine, he was a wonderful husband."

"Not good enough though," whispered Miranda.

Sean heard her comment and stared at her. "No man's ever good enough, is he?"

"Calm down, calm down," Abby piped up. "We all know Sean was wonderful to Raine."

Edward scoffed. "That's the story these girls tell each other. But if Sean was so good to her, why was my daughter at the casino, night after night? Where was he then? What was he doing? How could he allow something like that to go on?"

"That's a fair question," Chief Tan answered.

"I was at church," Sean interjected, "taking care of the community's needs."

"You were leaving my daughter alone, letting her buckle under," Edward snapped.

"Her father blames me for his own rotten treatment of Raine," Sean shouted. "But I'm sick of it."

"Not sick enough," Edward scoffed harder.

"Why don't you blame your own daughter for taking a lover?" Sean glared at him then.

"Because Raine would never do that, it didn't happen," Edward insisted.

"Oh no? There he is over there." Sean pointed violently to Victor. "Take a look. Exhibit Number One."

Victor fidgeted under the scrutiny and made fists at his side.

"I refuse to believe this man was her lover," Edward retorted. "It's a huge lie. Raine is being set up to be the guilty one. They're trying to make an excuse for why she disappeared. There's more to it, though. Much more, believe me."

Victor turned to the door and looked as if he were about to bolt.

"Do you have something you want to say?" Officer Tan stopped him.

"Not yet, not now," Victor spat out.

"How much money are they paying you for going along with this story?" Edward yelled at Victor then. "You're a patsy, fella, you're being had."

Victor rubbed his hands up and down his arms fiercely. "No one's paid me a cent, old fella! Not these idiots, or your crazy daughter. Your daughter made her own lousy choices and paid the price for it."

"Paid what price? Paid with her life?" Olivia couldn't keep silent.

The room grew deeply silent.

"You blaming me now too?" Victor turned threateningly to Olivia. "I knew you would the minute I saw you. I know your type."

"You don't know me at all." Olivia got into the fray.

"Yeah, yeah," Victor muttered. "All you gals who look so uptight and pretty, underneath you're the worst. Especially Raine."

"I'll kill you with my very own hands." Edward lunged at Victor then as Wayne jumped up and pulled him back.

Abby also ran over to Edward then, unable to take another moment of this.

"Edward, Edward, calm down, please. It won't do anyone any good if you have a heart attack, will it?" she pleaded.

"You're right, you're right," Edward conceded. "But don't worry, I'll have big news soon. And the minute I do, all the right people will land in the clinker. Forever."

Chief of Police Tan stood up abruptly. "The minute you have news, let us know, Edward," he said. "Otherwise, for now, we'll take a breather. A heavy wind storm's coming onto the island soon. The winds are already increasing. It's best that everybody go back to their rooms until it passes."

Miranda went boldly over to Victor then and stood beside him. "Let's go," she said loudly for all to hear, whisking him by the arm out of the room with her.

"Horrible," breathed Nessa. "This guy's a creep and she's the worst of the worst."

"Let's take a break now," Wayne repeated. "So far this has been very productive."

"What's the point of taking a break now?" Olivia whispered to Wayne as the room emptied out and they were left there together.

"Chief Tan has his reasons," Wayne said under his breath.

"What?" Olivia was confused.

"Listen, the wind's blowing up big time now," Wayne responded. "Let's go to the Villa Armene, around the corner. We can wait out the storm and talk. It should pass in a couple of hours."

*

The Villa Armene was a strange, low building made of yellow stucco, with a dark burgundy velvet cocktail lounge. A Mexican restaurant sat across from it and upstairs were small rooms to rent by the night. When Olivia walked in the first thing she noticed was a musky, dank feeling about it.

Wayne smiled, looking at her reaction. "Not exactly my first choice," he said. "It's just close to the station and I expect we'll be called back there shortly."

"Fine," said Olivia, slipping into a curving booth that had seen better days.

Wayne ordered warm drinks for them and put his head suddenly back along the booth.

"Tired?" asked Olivia.

"Not tired, just not hopeful," Wayne murmured slowly. "Too many dysfunctional friends and family. I've seen it over and over. If you get pulled into their trip you can suspect one after another for everything. You've got to be careful or your imagination will run wild."

Olivia was glad to hear that because it was exactly what was happening to her. Several of them could be responsible for Raine's disappearance, she thought. There had been enough jealousy and bitterness in the room to fuel all kinds of reactions. One of them certainly could have brought Raine to harm.

"Do you think one of them killed her?" Olivia ventured as the warm drinks were brought to them and the wind outside blew harder.

"We can't go there without evidence." Wayne picked his drink up right away. "It's tempting to speculate, but I say, don't."

Olivia didn't get it. "Isn't that what detectives do, though? Don't we have to speculate and then check out what we think?"

"We have to follow the trail of solid evidence," Wayne replied. "Or else we get detoured, spend our entire time chasing fantasies that lead nowhere, fast."

That was an interesting way of putting it. Olivia liked it.

"I'm actually relieved that Raine's father hired private investigators, though," she said, finishing her drink.

"I know you are," Wayne replied. "It's not necessarily a good thing, though. Private investigators can complicate matters, get in the way of what we're doing if they don't coordinate with us. As far as I know, these investigators haven't coordinated. Edward's done this on his own!"

"That's why Chief Tan called off the meeting?" Olivia asked.

"Most likely," said Wayne. "Tan had to check on who these investigators were and what cards they were holding, first."

Olivia was still glad other investigators were on the case. And she also needed to sort out her own thoughts about it as well. This was a good time to talk to Wayne about it.

"From where I'm sitting," Olivia started, "it seems as though Miranda stole away Raine's lover. That much is obvious!"

"No, it isn't." Wayne stopped her. "We don't know that. It's possible Victor was seeing Miranda first and Raine was the one who stole him away, isn't it?"

"Either way, that makes Miranda a suspect, doesn't it? Miranda has to be happy that Raine is out of the picture now." Olivia was quick on the uptake.

"Not necessarily," Wayne replied. "That's based on assumption. For all we know, Miranda and Victor just met. For all we know, Raine knew nothing of it. Maybe Miranda is just having fun and the relationship doesn't mean that much to her, either. If she were looking for something serious, it's doubtful she'd choose someone like Victor, isn't it?"

Olivia couldn't help but agree. "Well, what about Victor, then?" she plunged forward. "The guy seems like he could be a psychopath."

"What do you base that on?" Wayne seemed uneasy.

"When I spoke to Victor about Raine's disappearance in the club, he didn't show much reaction, "said Olivia. "In fact, he actually said he didn't care, thought Raine was playing some kind of game."

"It's possible he's right, isn't it?" Wayne's voice got louder.

"Sure, anything's possible." Olivia felt strengthened. "But now Victor's out with someone else, so quickly! Creepy to say the least."

Wayne laughed. "Creepy doesn't make the guy a psychopath," he retorted. "It could just make him a guy that played around with a married woman and got in over his head. There's no evidence yet that Victor's done anything criminal. There's evidence that he and Raine fought, but no other abuse of any kind has been reported. We checked his records and he's come up clean, except for one small burglary a few years ago."

"A burglary's something!" Olivia was jarred to hear it, and also jarred by Wayne's nonchalant attitude.

"A burglary's unrelated to what's going on now," Wayne responded. "Though, to tell the truth, Chief Tan seems to be on your side. He's uncomfortable with how Victor's reacting, but we can't do a thing about it right now."

"Good." Olivia felt vindicated that someone else agreed with her. "I can't wait to hear what Edward's private Investigators come up with," she breathed.

"I wouldn't count on that either." Wayne put his hand on Olivia's briefly, to calm her down. "I know Raine was your good friend, but at this point, really, you have to start letting go."

"Letting go of Raine?" Olivia was horrified. "Just letting her vanish like smoke? Never knowing what happened to her?"

"That's how most missing person's cases turn out," Wayne reminded her.

"No, it's impossible! Can't be done!" Olivia refused it.

Wayne shook his head sadly. "Then just let go of the hope that we'll find anything much more to go on right now. If we find it, great. But don't expect it."

"You're pessimistic," Olivia replied.

"Realistic," Wayne replied. "You know I'm a restorative justice guy. I've seen too many wrongful convictions. I'd rather give it a long time before I nail anyone. Someone can look as guilty as hell and come up smelling of roses. And the opposite, as well."

"Okay, I get what you're saying." Olivia respected his fair-minded attitude. "It's a good way to be. An abundance of caution."

"Thank you." Wayne seemed relieved. "And will you please go tell Lorna that too? She hates my attitude, considers me passive. We're opposites on this point."

Olivia realized that.

"In fact," Wayne continued, "it's getting so bad Lorna and I may have to part ways."

Olivia was surprised to actually hear that. "Sorry," she said. "That has to be hard."

"Me, too," replied Wayne, "very sorry."

114

"It could actually be better for both of you in the long run, though, if there's too much friction," Olivia offered.

"Yeah, I guess it could." Wayne seemed disturbed by the thought of it though.

"You care for Lorna?" Olivia asked quietly, seeing his upset.

"Of course I do," Wayne shot back. "If you don't care for your partner you can't work together as a real team."

"Of course not," Olivia agreed as the winds blew harder and Wayne's phone lit up with a message.

Wayne grabbed it, picked up, listened, and immediately got pale.

CHAPTER TWENTY

"What's happening?" Olivia asked, breathless.

"Okay," Wayne muttered. "Okay, got it." Then he looked up at Olivia. "You were right. I was wrong."

"Right about what?" she demanded.

"The big tip is in!" Wayne replied. "Edward's private investigators have spread out. They've also been in Key Largo."

"They found her there?" Olivia's heart started pounding. She felt stunned and thrilled at the same time.

"Not exactly, but Raine was just spotted on surveillance cameras at the beach of a small hotel. She was swimming there the night after the party, with Victor."

"With Victor?" Olivia was stunned.

"Victor," Wayne replied.

Olivia felt a burst of excitement, mixed with dread. "Does it mean she's in Key Largo now?"

"Not necessarily," Wayne countered immediately.

"What was she doing on the cameras?" Olivia felt breathless.

"Swimming with Victor," Wayne repeated.

Something didn't sit right with Olivia, but she wasn't sure just what yet. She knew that Victor and Raine had been in a relationship. She hadn't heard that they'd broken up yet. Olivia wracked her brain to see what was bothering her about this. Then it came to her.

"Wait a minute," Olivia exclaimed, "Victor told me he hadn't seen Raine after the bachelorette party. I specifically asked him twice to be sure!"

"That's right." Wayne confirmed it. "He said the same thing to Chief Tan when we talked to him. We have it on record."

"Oh my God." Olivia grew silent. "He's lied on the record. Something's terribly wrong."

"Yes, it is," Wayne conceded. "And it's more than a lie. Now Victor's officially the last person to see Raine before she disappeared. Finally, we have something specific."

"What could Raine have been thinking?" Olivia breathed. "She didn't go back up to Miami as she said, she headed down to be with Victor again that night in Key Largo."

"That much is clear," said Wayne.

"What did she go down there for?" Olivia began to speculate. "They were in a fight and she might have wanted to make up with him."

"Possible," Wayne agreed.

"More than that," Olivia mused out loud. "Raine was attached to him, she needed him. Looks like she couldn't stay away from him." Olivia's words fell all over one another.

"I wouldn't go that far," said Wayne.

"Does Miranda know about this?"

"That's a good question," Wayne responded. "I don't have the answer. I know that Sean and Edward have been informed. They're beside themselves, both of them."

"I can only imagine," breathed Olivia.

"Edward's on the war path and Sean refuses to say a word. Anyway, Chief Tan arranged for a bunch of us to head down to Key Largo now. The beach at the hotel Raine was swimming at is near a popular underwater wreck. Tourists visit it regularly, it's a well-known diving site."

Olivia was terrified. "You think she and Victor dove down and he killed her and left her body there?"

"Anything is possible." Wayne now also seemed nervous. "There are divers there now, looking for her. We also have to search the island carefully. Tan's already sent Key Largo police out to scan the area. This is big! It will be all over the news."

Olivia felt chills racing through her body. "Victor has to know where Raine is," she breathed. "For all we know, maybe Miranda does too."

"I don't know about Miranda, but Victor definitely knows more than he's letting on," Wayne agreed. "Actually, the police are taking him in as we speak."

"How long can they hold him?" Olivia wanted to speak to Victor again in jail. She wanted to stare him down and demand he tell her what happened to her friend.

"For a little while," Wayne answered. "Victor's definitely a person of interest now."

"Why would he do this, though?" Olivia asked. "What could he possibly get out of it? Did Raine drive him past his limit? Was there more that went on between them than meets the eye? Or is Miranda behind this?"

"Or someone else?" Wayne added.

Olivia couldn't think of anyone else at the moment who could be involved.

"What does any killer get out of their crime?" Wayne continued. "A sense of power, control, a momentary thrill?"

"The belief that the crime will be hidden forever?" echoed Olivia.

"Some enjoy seeing the pain they're causing," Wayne added. "They live off the torment of others, like a brutal scavenger living off garbage."

Olivia closed her eyes. For some odd reason, Victor didn't fit that description to her. He seemed too strong and grounded in who he was, distasteful though it might be.

"Okay, you're coming with us, of course?" Wayne added then.

"Down to Key Largo? Of course," said Olivia quickly. "No place else I'd be. Who else is coming?"

"Sean's coming and Raine's father," Wayne added.

"That sounds like a recipe for disaster," Olivia commented. "How are they going to handle it?"

"They both want to come. There's no way we can refuse them," Wayne commented. "It's Sean's wife, and Edward's daughter. In case Raine turns up, they need to be there."

"But they hate each other like poison," Olivia added.

"They'll keep it together now. They have to," Wayne added. "We have no time to be sidetracked. And besides, now they each have Victor to blame."

*

Wayne, Olivia, Sean, and Edward piled into a Jeep along with two other officers and as the light started to fade headed down the beautiful highway near the ocean to Key Largo. The open sky and rippling waters were an odd accompaniment to the frenzy in the car.

"It's just like her, it's just like her," Edward kept muttering in the back seat.

Sean, pale and agitated, sat near the opposite car window, his hands completely clenched.

"Drive faster," Edward yelled. "She could run away if she gets wind that we're coming."

Sean began tapping the windowpane. "She's not running anywhere, Ed," he muttered glumly, startling both Edward and Olivia.

"You don't know that, creep!" Edward lashed back at him.

"What do you mean?" Olivia asked Sean.

"I meant Raine will be glad when we get there," said Sean. "Why would she run away? For all we know Victor's got her holed up somewhere, has been blackmailing her for all she's worth."

"She ran from you before, didn't she?" Edward snapped back. "She ran to the bachelorette party and then she came down here

118

with that lousy guy. Some women go from bad to worse, like Raine's mother. I never thought Raine would too."

Olivia looked through the mirror at Sean in the back seat. He was doing his absolute best not to take the bait.

"Ed's tremendously upset." Olivia turned to Sean, trying to soothe him.

"He's always upset." Sean's eyes were glassy. "And I always take the brunt of it."

"Quiet down, guys," one of the officers in the rear interrupted. "This is rough for everyone. We'll all be better off if we quiet down."

Sean nodded and Edward mumbled something Olivia couldn't make out. She decided to engage Sean in conversation anyway, take his attention away from Edward.

"Does Miranda know Raine and Victor were seen on the video swimming together?" she asked Sean.

"How do I know?" he snapped back. "I have no idea. I can ask Sloane if you want me to. Why?"

"That's a good idea," Olivia continued. "It seems Miranda and Victor are dating. I wonder how Miranda would take to the news about Raine being sighted swimming with Victor at the hotel that night."

"I've given up wondering how Raine's friends would react to things," Sean promptly replied. "Sloane is the most stable. The rest of them go hot and cold depending on what's happening."

"Including Raine?" Wayne chimed in.

"Why should she be any different?" Sean said between clenched teeth.

Sean's comment surprised Olivia. This was the first time he'd ever said anything disparaging about Raine.

"You do whatever you can for a woman," Sean went on, "then you have to let the chips fall where they may."

"If you're doing all you can for a woman," Edward interjected, "the chips stay right at home. She doesn't run off with scum and go for a late-night swim at a sleazy hotel. Raine deserves better than that."

Sean had enough. In a flash he spun around and turned to Edward. "Maybe Raine didn't feel she deserved better than that, though," he said. "Maybe a person gets just what they deserve."

"Exactly what do you mean by that?" Edward's eyes were fluttering with pain. "You're saying my daughter deserved to go missing, to be out there somewhere alone in the night, terrified?"

Sean shut up quickly then and wouldn't say another word as the Jeep suddenly veered off the highway onto the first exit to Key Largo.

CHAPTER TWENTY ONE

As the Jeep drove further off the exit, Key Largo spread out before them. The island was home to tropical hardwoods, winding creeks, state parks, and a marine sanctuary, and visitors flocked here naturally. A famous underwater wreck was close to the beach Raine had been swimming at and also a coral reef park and a botanical park. There were plenty of places that she could be hiding. Olivia wracked her brain, trying to think of the most outlandish possibilities.

Could Raine be alive right now, wandering around with tourists? Did something happen to her, and she forgot who she was? Olivia suddenly remembered a time in college when Raine drank so much, she hit her head and couldn't remember who she was for two days. The memory chilled Olivia. My God, had that happened again? Olivia paused and immediately realized it was unlikely. Raine's photo had been plastered all over the place. If she was right out there in public, someone would recognize her.

"We're going straight to the hotel Raine was spotted at," Wayne announced as they drove closer. "Investigators have been there all afternoon speaking to people both at the hotel and around the area."

"Good work," said Olivia, relieved at least to be near the place where Raine was last seen alive.

"We have rooms waiting for us at the hotel," Wayne continued. "After we check in we can scan the place, talk to local police and private investigators. The news has hit all over TV. Posters are being handed out and the locals are on high alert."

"Something will turn up soon, I'm positive," Edward exclaimed. "It's just like Raine to leave something behind to tell us where she is."

Sean shuddered. "I've called the pastor of our church for prayers," he reported. "By now everyone in the world knows about Raine and Victor. It's humiliating, to say the least."

"It's going to be okay, Sean," Wayne tried to soothe him.

"No, it won't," Sean responded. "Nothing will ever be okay again."

The Jeep drove up to a low, sprawling hotel beside a small beach then and pulled into the driveway. One after another they got out. Edward stumbled out of the car last, looking lost and forlorn.

*

After they checked into their rooms they all met outside on the small veranda of the hotel, overlooking the beach. It was dark out now, just as it had been when Raine was last seen on it. A few stars had appeared in the sky and you could hear the sound of the waves gently lapping against the shore. They looked at each other silently, taking it in. Was this what Raine saw in her last moments on earth? Was she still somewhere, alive, waiting to be rescued?

The police officers who had traveled with them spoke first. "We're heading over to the station to get briefed now," one of them said. "Then we'll join the search and report whatever we hear back to Officer Tan immediately."

"Good," Wayne said approvingly. "Olivia and I are going to speak to other investigators on the case now. We'll see what they've found and what next steps are needed."

Sean and Edward cast a disheartening glance at one another.

"I'm catching up with the head of my team now," Edward reported. "He asked me to meet him privately at Shore Drive as soon as I got here."

Olivia wondered if there might be more information that hadn't come out. "Will you let us know what he says immediately?" she asked Edward.

Edward looked at Olivia strangely. "Maybe I will and maybe not. Depends what he tells me. There's no promises here."

Olivia didn't like that, and was about to reply when Sean tugged her hand. He was trying to tell Olivia to leave it alone, let Edward do what he had to.

"I guess that leaves you, Sean." Wayne turned to him.

"I'll just stay here at the hotel in the lobby and pick up whatever I can," Sean said disconsolately.

Olivia felt uneasy about that. Sean would probably end up talking to guests who might have seen Raine and Victor here together. It would rough for him to hear. No telling how he'd react.

"Are you up for that, Sean?" Olivia asked, concerned. "Who knows what people will say?"

"I'm up for anything at this point," Sean replied. "What's worse than what's happened by now?"

Olivia felt uneasy leaving Sean behind. Underneath his calm exterior, she could feel him smoldering.

Each of them turned to go in their separate directions then. "Maybe we should take Sean with us?" Olivia suggested to Wayne.

"We can't," replied Wayne. "This is strictly professional. The detectives won't talk to us if Sean is around."

Olivia and Wayne walked around to the back of the hotel, where the police and assorted investigators had set up headquarters in a small room.

Wayne knocked at the door briskly and then turned the knob. Fortunately, the door was open. He and Olivia walked in.

The room was small, airless, and musty with a large clock on the wall. Two men sat at a small round table, drinking coffee, and looked up slowly as Wayne and Olivia walked in.

"We've been expecting you," one of them said. "Detective Ben Parrish here, and this is my buddy Dan."

"Thanks for waiting for us," Wayne said immediately as he pulled up two small folding chairs that stood on the side and placed them around the table. "Okay, fill us in."

Ben laughed a second. "You act like we hit a gold mine, we didn't. There's not so much to fill you in on. Only the usual stuff."

"What's usual?" Olivia asked. Ben's voice had a tone of scorn in it that she didn't like.

"A slimy guy and supposedly classy woman get it on down here in the Keys," Ben responded. "It's not exactly big news."

"It is big news when the woman goes missing, though." Wayne didn't seem to like Ben's attitude either.

"That's true." Ben rubbed his heavy face. "It's just hot and we're tired. It's been a long day."

The other detective, Dan, took over immediately then. He spoke simply and respectfully. Olivia felt better listening to him.

"Most of the people we talked to who saw Victor and Raine said they seemed fine," Dan reported. "They seemed happy, having a good time. They were seen laughing, dancing in the club and also spotted going together for that late-night swim."

"A swim near the underwater wreck?" Olivia asked abruptly.

"Good question. I didn't hear that," Dan replied, smiling at Olivia approvingly. "The two of them were also caught on the surveillance video swimming at the beach that night. The video didn't show which part of the beach exactly."

"And after the swim, what then?" Wayne was all over it. "Any videos of Victor returning alone?"

"No, nothing like that," said Dan.

"There had to be some shots of them coming out of the water?" Wayne demanded.

"There weren't," Dan replied. "They could have come out at another part of the beach. We've been trying like crazy to trace Victor's footsteps that night. No luck. It was too late, no one saw him."

"Someone had to see him check out of the hotel the next morning then?" Olivia jumped in. "Or check out later that night? If he stayed around, someone had to see him alone the next day."

"There's express checkout at the hotel." Dan shook his head. "And no one saw him again after that night."

"That's not good." Wayne stood up abruptly.

"They could have gone somewhere else after the swim?" Ben chimed in. "Just because no one saw him alone doesn't add up to much."

"It definitely does, it's irregular." Wayne's eyes flashed. "And besides, we've got more than that. Victor's been caught in an out and out lie. He said he never saw Raine the night after the bachelorette party. He told that to Olivia and also to the police."

"I heard that," Dan quickly agreed.

Ben shrugged. "So he lied about spending another night with a married lady? Big deal."

"It's a big deal when the lady goes missing, Ben," Dan repeated.

"When and where was Victor spotted again?" Wayne needed to know immediately.

"We found out that he turned up in Miami the next day," said Dan.

"Miami?" Wayne flushed. "Victor lives in Key West! What in hell was he doing in Miami?"

"He goes to the casino up there from time to time, as well as the one in Key West," Ben chimed in. "People up there know him."

"Raine went to both casinos, too," Olivia murmured. "Were she and Victor seen at the casino in Miami in the past together?"

"Good question," said Dan.

"Victor was up in the casino in Miami without Raine the next day," Wayne was summarizing. "Just checking to be sure."

"Yes, that's right," said Ben. "This video on the beach is the last time anyone saw them together."

"Or saw her at all." Wayne was restless, going over and over evidence as if he were chewing on a bone. "It's odd that Victor was back up in Raine's hometown without her, the day after she goes missing. He must have gone up there to collect money. Why else would he go?"

"Could be," Dan agreed.

"To collect something! The question is what?" Olivia chimed in.

"You think he was part of a hit was put out on Raine?" Dan focused in.

Ben shook his head again then. "A hit? By who? Why? There's no evidence of it. For all we know Raine sent Victor up to the casino in Miami herself. She could be holed up somewhere down here waiting for him to bring the money to her. For all we know he delivered it already and she used it to escape."

That was an interesting theory and it struck Olivia immediately. Victor would then just be the middleman in a chain.

"Could have, would have." Wayne was uneasy. "There's no time left for speculation. It's always the money trail. I myself went to the casino in Miami to talk to Dupris a few days ago."

Ben stood up beside Wayne. "Dupris hightailed it out of town," he muttered.

"Yes, he did," said Wayne. "He left a day or so before. Did he know what was coming? Dupris held Raine's debts. Some people think they might even be together. I'd say that's unlikely, seeing what's going on between Raine and Victor."

"It doesn't mean Dupris's not still involved," said Olivia.

"What did Victor say he was doing at the casino in Miami the next day?" Wayne was becoming more and more distressed. "Why wasn't Raine with him? Where did she go?"

"I heard that Victor was grilled about that a few hours ago," Ben reported. "He said after the night in Key Largo, Raine wanted to stay down there a little longer. He left and decided to go to Miami."

"Why?" Wayne was insistent.

"Victor said he had a friend to talk to in Miami, that's all," said Ben.

"Who's the friend? What did they talk about? We have to check anyone who saw him at the casino and see what they know," Wayne added briskly.

"It's all in the works," Dan added, giving Olivia a long glance. "I heard you were Raine's good friend," he added. "I'm sorry."

"Yes, that's right, I was," Olivia replied. "And I still am. Always will be."

*

"We have to run this by Sean right away," Wayne said, as he and Olivia left Ben and Dan. "How much did Sean know about what went on with Olivia at the casino in Miami, really? So far he says not much. People there said he never showed up. She usually was there alone. And we still haven't found out who paid her debts.

Was Edward still coughing up the money? Or did Victor find someone to pay them for her?"

That was hard to imagine, but it could have been. "I'd be careful talking to Sean," Olivia replied. "He's really on edge right now. Sean's become a man with nothing more to lose, he can't take too much more at the moment."

Wayne sighed deeply. "It'll all come together before long," he said under his breath. "I feel it. We're right on the edge of getting that one piece of information that will pull these loose pieces together."

Olivia felt that as well. "Listen, let me talk to Sean myself," she said to Wayne. "I'm working for him, after all. He might feel easier speaking to me right now."

"Sure, go for it." Wayne was pleased with the suggestion. "Go find him at the hotel and talk to him before you go to bed. Do it tonight when he's edgy and tired. That's our best shot of having him let it rip and talk to us straight."

CHAPTER TWENTY TWO

To Olivia's surprise, when she returned to the hotel she found Sean sitting outside on the veranda alone, looking at the darkened sky.

"Can I join you a moment?" Olivia asked as she approached him.

"Whatever," Sean answered, not turning to greet her.

Olivia sat down quietly, not wanting to intrude upon Sean's privacy.

"This must be very hard for you," she said finally.

"You got that right," Sean responded curtly.

"I'm so sorry," Olivia offered.

"I've been publicly taken for a fool," Sean went on, his voice filled with both sadness and fury. "How is this going to look to the people who work for our charities?"

Olivia could understand his concern. "If we find Raine alive, perhaps she can explain?"

"If we find her alive? Has it gotten to that point?" Sean's voice grew darker. "The police found evidence that she's dead?"

"No, they haven't," Olivia backtracked.

"Well, let's not go there then," Sean barked. "Let's not flood the news with more gore than they already have on their plate. They love that stuff, eat it up. Everyone loves to see good people crumbling, don't they?"

"Some," Olivia commented.

"Most," Sean replied.

Olivia sympathized with how Sean was feeling. She'd been through the shock of finding out awful things about a partner herself. Your whole world starts collapsing then, she understood. Olivia longed to ask Sean a few questions, though.

"May I ask you a few questions?" she asked tentatively.

"No," Sean answered suddenly, startling Olivia. "I've told everyone the same thing over and over and it's made me look like a jerk. I said we had a happy marriage. I thought we did. I said I gave her everything she needed. Obviously, that wasn't true, either."

This wasn't the time to press him further and Olivia knew it. "Okay, I'll call it a night then," she said, standing suddenly.

Sean didn't like that, either. "Sit down! Now you're going to run away too? You can't take the truth?"

"Of course I can take the truth," Olivia replied. "It just seems you prefer to be by yourself now. You said you didn't want to answer questions."

"That's right," said Sean, "but it doesn't mean I don't want to talk."

Olivia sat back down gingerly, letting him take the lead.

"Raine's a good woman," he began speaking slowly. "Something happened to her. I'm sitting here trying to figure it out. I have no idea how it all ended like this. Life jumps on you from behind when no one's looking."

Olivia found Sean's words heart-wrenching. She could certainly relate.

"Yes, it does," she replied. "It happened to me, too."

"I know it did," Sean said, "that's why I wanted you on the case."

"Thank you," said Raine. "I really appreciate being involved."

"I know you do," said Sean. "Just let me say one thing to you, though, back off a little. Take it slow."

Olivia was startled. "Why? We have to find her."

"I don't mean that," Sean replied. "Sure, we have to find her, but don't let the police and detectives draw you into the filth. This is filth we're looking at now! Just filth. It has nothing to do with what happened to Raine."

"Maybe it does," said Olivia. As she strained to look over at Sean, she saw the veins in his neck protruding and his hands clenched together in his lap. It had to be especially hard for someone who was so prominent for his good works to endure something like this.

"Filth, filth," Sean kept murmuring.

"I don't call it filth, Sean, I call it life," Olivia responded. "It happens to all of us sooner or later."

"Not to all of us," he responded. "Not to me and mine!"

*

After a few more moments, Olivia left Sean sitting there and went up to her small, slanty room. Fortunately, she had left the windows open wide and a soft breeze was blowing in. After changing into a light nightgown, Olivia fell into bed. The day had been long and exhausting. It was strangely comforting, though, to realize that Raine had stayed right in this hotel. Maybe down the hall, even. What happened to her after she'd gone swimming? The thought filled Olivia's mind and wouldn't leave it.

Olivia closed her eyes then and felt sleep coming as the thoughts revolved around in her mind. Where was Raine now? Did she and Victor fight in the water? Did he drown her by accident? Had her body dropped deep into the ocean and been consumed by the life in it now?

Olivia fell into a strange fitful sleep then, with vivid dreams. In one dream she saw Raine standing on a hill, beautifully dressed, laughing.

"Raine," Olivia called out in the dream, only to see her quickly fade away.

A little while later, Olivia dreamt that she saw Raine sitting in a strange café, drinking coffee, waving at her.

Instead of waving back, Olivia awoke with a shock. What were these dreams? Was Raine gone and trying to reach her, telling her she had died? Or was she trying to say she was still close by? Olivia's heart started pounding wildly as she got out of bed and rushed to the open window.

"Raine," she called out, "where are you?"

But the only answer that came was silence. Silence and the blowing of the lonely breeze.

*

Olivia abruptly awoke early the next morning. She'd arranged to meet Wayne downstairs for breakfast, and despite being tired, didn't have the luxury of sleeping in. There were almost no breaks to be had while working a case. Olivia's life had become austere and disciplined. It was good for her, though, she realized. Strangely, she liked it this way.

Olivia showered quickly. One thing she loved about the work was that she never knew what the day was bringing. She slipped into a paisley, linen dress, pulled her hair behind her with a ribbon, and grabbed her bag. But just as Olivia was about to go out the door, her phone rang. No doubt it was Wayne checking on her, making sure she was on her way downstairs.

Olivia quickly picked up the phone. "Olivia, Olivia," Wayne was shouting.

Olivia's body froze. "What?"

"I'm glad you picked up immediately," Wayne was practically yelling.

"What is it? Tell me!"

"It's over. They found her!" Wayne burst out.

"Found Raine?" Olivia could barely get the words out.

"Her body washed up in a swamp a few miles away," Wayne added. "They found her at six a.m. this morning. I just got the news."

"Oh no, no," Olivia gasped.

"It's over," he repeated.

"Did she drown? Was she killed?" Olivia started crying.

"I can't say that for sure, yet." Wayne tried to compose himself. "It's possible she drowned. We'll find out soon, though. Right now they're collecting evidence and taking the body to the medical examiner."

"Body?" Olivia's alive, wonderful friend had turned into a body. This was no longer a missing person case.

"Come downstairs immediately," Wayne insisted.

"I'm on my way," Olivia barely breathed.

*

A crowd had already gathered outside the hotel when Olivia got down. The minute she arrived Wayne rushed over to her.

"Come on, we're going to the swamp," he breathed.

Olivia felt herself turn pale. "Is Raine's body still there? I want to see her, to say good-bye."

"I'm not sure," Wayne answered. "But everybody's down there now."

"Sean? Raine's father?" Olivia asked, speechless.

"No, not yet," Wayne said as he whisked Olivia into a small, dark car waiting for them at the curb. "Sean and Edward are just finding out. Detectives are with them now, talking to them in person. Only law enforcement are permitted at the swamp right now."

Wayne and Olivia slipped into the car and it sped off as if on a high-speed chase, down a few blocks, across a big highway and then toward the back of town.

"Where is this swamp? How did Raine get there?" Olivia breathed as they sped through Key Largo.

"It's at the back of the Key." Wayne was focused and methodical. "It's not a place you'd go swimming in. Seems most likely her body was dumped."

"Dumped? My God, why? By who?"

"Or it could have floated through the ocean and washed up there," Wayne mused.

"Are they sure it's Raine? She's definitely dead?" Olivia couldn't help ask as the car got closer.

Wayne grabbed Olivia's hand and squeezed it. "There's no doubt about it," he murmured. "I'm really very sorry."

*

The swamp was cordoned off with long, yellow ribbons when Olivia and Wayne arrived. It was hidden under thick brush, down a sloping hill, not far from an inlet. Wayne showed his identification to an officer there and the two of them were quickly let in.

Lots of officers were sprawled out all over the place, taking photos and picking up whatever evidence they could find. Olivia hoped she could see Raine one more time. And she also hoped she could not. She was terrified to see Raine's body and whatever may have been done to it. She was also relieved that Sean and Edward were not here now.

There was a sickening smell as they got down closer to the muddy water. Olivia wanted to put her hands over her eyes and hold her breath. This was a place where everything festered; all kinds of insects crawled underfoot, mosquitoes buzzed, and the sound of a strange bird rang out.

"Is she still here?" Olivia asked, breathless.

"I don't know yet," said Wayne. "We'll see in a minute."

"How did she get here?" Olivia had a thousand questions piling over one another in her mind.

"The ocean could have swept her up here," Wayne said as he looked the place over. "Or she could have died in the water somewhere else and been washed up on shore."

"I can't stay here long." Olivia shivered as Wayne put his hand on her shoulder.

"It's okay, we won't have to," he said. "We just have to get a good look at the place ourselves. You never know what you'll find at the site of a murder or where a body is found."

Olivia wondered what he expected.

"The body itself is a treasure trove information too," Wayne continued, "and sometimes there's something on the body, or that falls close by that gives us just what we're looking for."

Olivia knew that Wayne was looking for hard evidence. He'd need it to put her killer away.

As they walked further into the center of the area, Olivia looked around wildly to see if Raine was still close by. Was she waiting for them to come and say good-bye to her?

Wayne stopped and watched Olivia. "The body's gone," he said quietly. "Looks like they've already taken it to the medical examiner."

Olivia was gripped with a feeling of missing Raine terribly. She started to cry softly. They hadn't seen each other for such a long time. And now they never would again.

"It's good that the body's not here," Wayne whispered. "It means they're all over it. There's a ton of publicity on this case and they want to get news out quickly."

"The news is out already." Olivia caught her breath.

"I mean they need to let the public know whether or not this is a homicide," Wayne said. "And if it is, they've got to make sure a killer is not still roaming around."

"They'll know that right away?" Olivia felt chilled again.

"Sometimes it's obvious. Other times, not," said Wayne.

"Good thing you have Victor in custody," Olivia added.

"Very good," Wayne agreed.

"But you need hard evidence to convict, don't you?" Olivia reminded him.

"Yes, we do," Wayne answered. "And most of the time the body has it for us. Now that Raine's turned up, we're in a completely different ball park."

Olivia and Wayne wandered around the swamp area and spent time looking over the rocks, mud, and twigs that lay around it. Wayne focused carefully on everything around. It was as if he almost hoped something had dropped out of Raine's pocket that would tell him what had happened to her. But Olivia could think of nothing else but that her friend had washed up here, lifeless and alone. Her body had actually been a few feet away from where Olivia was standing. Was there some way Raine knew that Olivia was here now, trying to help her?

Wayne took a few steps away from Olivia then and walked over to a heavy officer who'd been digging through the mud. The officer seemed to know Wayne, and the two of them talked confidentially. Wayne nodded his head a few times and Olivia wondered what he was learning. She'd find out soon enough. And soon they'd have to go back to the hotel and confront everyone there, friends, family, reporters, and especially Edward and Sean. The horror and finality gripped Olivia. Where would she go from here?

Wayne shook hands with the officer suddenly and seemed to thank him. Then he walked back to Olivia.

"It's okay, we can go back to the hotel now," said Wayne.

Olivia looked at him searchingly. "You got what you needed?"

"It's a good beginning," Wayne said. "Looks like we've got a definite homicide on our hands. He said it was pretty clear that Raine's head had been bashed in with a rock."

Olivia began shivering tremendously. "My God, my God."

"It's awful, I know it." Wayne tried to comfort Olivia. "But it's over now. She's not in pain anymore."

"How do you know that?" Olivia bristled.

"At least I hope she's not," Wayne said softly.

"Okay, let's go back to the hotel for now. More details will be filled in quickly," said Wayne. "The hotel is where we're needed now."

CHAPTER TWENTY THREE

When Olivia and Wayne got back to the hotel the crowd gathered around it was even larger than before. Local photographers and assorted reporters from all kinds of venues were spread around, snapping pictures and talking to guests. Olivia wondered how Sean and Edward were doing. She could barely imagine. It all felt like a dream.

Wayne led Olivia silently through the crowd, up to the lobby. The investigation was quickly tightening up. Wayne had been informed that Police Chief Tan would be there waiting for them. As soon as they walked in, he was right at the door.

"Okay," Officer Tan said grimly, pulling them over to the side. "Definitely looks like a homicide. Of course we have to get the official word from the medical examiner before we can give the information out. That will happen shortly. We also have to be sure we get the killer locked up! The people out there are now nervous."

"You got Victor," Olivia commented.

"Yes, looks like it," Chief Tan replied, "but we don't have enough on him yet."

"Has Victor been informed that her body has washed up?" asked Wayne. "How's he reacting?"

"Victor's showing reaction, playing it dumb," said Chief Tan. "He says Raine was fine when he left her."

"Left her where?" asked Olivia, disturbed. "Swimming in the water? No one saw her alive again after that."

"At least we can hold him longer now," Chief Tan added.

"Is there any evidence the body was dumped?" Wayne went on. "Are there any footprints in or near the swamp?"

"Doesn't look like it," said Chief Tan, "but we're not ready to say no definitely. If Raine was dumped, the killer was a professional who knew just what he was doing. He covered all traces from bottom to top."

"Important to know that," mused Wayne.

"It does look like it was a crime of passion though," Chief Tan continued. "Her head was definitely bashed in by a rock. A violent death, fueled by rage and hate."

Olivia winced.

"She probably had another fight with that low-life when they were swimming in the water," Tan continued. "He lost it, bashed her, and let her dead body drown. I'm sure he never thought anyone would find her. Only the body washed up. It's happened before. The body can have a mind of its own."

The scenario being painted chilled Olivia to the core. "How are going to prove Victor did that?" she asked haltingly.

Officer Tan looked over at her. "That's the question, isn't it? We've got to get him to spill the beans. In the absence of that, we need as much supportive, circumstantial evidence as we can find."

"We've got plenty already," Wayne jumped in. "Victor lied about when he last saw her. He said he never saw her after the night of bachelorette party. But she was last seen alive with him on the video the next night. There's also a confirmed report they had a fight the night of that party. That was a day before she disappeared. Victor's also dating Raine's good friend Miranda."

"Yeah, that leads to motive!" Tan added. "Could be Raine became too much for them and he wanted to get rid of her to be with this other gal. Or Raine found out about him and Miranda and she and Miranda had a fight? For all we know Miranda pushed Victor to handle it and get rid of Raine for good. You'd be amazed how often something like that happens."

Olivia's head began to spin as she went over her meeting with Miranda. Originally, Miranda had not told Olivia about Raine and Victor. She had to have known about it but had said nothing. It was Sloane who had mentioned Victor to Olivia. Miranda had actually sent Olivia in a different direction, trying to point suspicion at Sloane.

"We're going to have to really grill Miranda." Chief Tan rubbed his foot on the floor. "She's got to be plenty scared now, they all are. If Miranda's got more on Victor, she'll tell us, if we play it right."

Wayne turned to Olivia. "I think it's best to let Olivia do this. It will be less threatening to Miranda than having the police pull her in. Olivia knows Miranda anyway. They met up in Miami."

"Good call," said Chief Tan.

"I want to speak to Sean as well," Olivia blurted out, "and also Edward. How are they doing?"

"They're freaked out," said Chief Tan. "Everyone is. It's to be expected. Lots of friends and family are on the way down now, too. Including Sean's pastor, Emory Harris. He's known Raine and Sean for years. Harris has issued some kind of statement to the papers saying what great people Raine and Sean are."

"Did Harris also know about Raine's gambling addiction and relationship with Victor?" Wayne was quick on the draw.

"Doubtful." Chief Tan shook his head slowly. "But who knows? It's probably a good idea for Olivia to talk to the pastor, too. You never know where the final word comes from."

Olivia breathed deeply. She was needed here now and she knew it. She had to straighten up, be calm and steady. She couldn't afford herself the luxury of falling apart or grieving. A flash of steel strength shot up through her then, though she had no idea where it came from.

"Okay, I'm on it," Olivia said with such resolve, it startled both Wayne and Chief Tan.

"Good for you." Chief Tan smiled a second.

"When is Miranda coming down here?" Olivia asked.

"She'll be here in about an hour," Chief Tan replied. "Start with her first. Since she's got something going with Victor, she's the best bet. In the meantime, go get yourself some breakfast and rest. It's gonna be a long day, you can bet on that."

"It already has been," Olivia replied, "one of the longest of my life." Yet to Olivia's surprise she was ready to go full force ahead and handle whatever came along.

*

About an hour later Olivia went down to the back patio of the hotel, which had been turned over to the investigation. Miranda sat on it, sobbing.

"My God, my God, how did this happen?" she asked Olivia.

Olivia went over and sat down beside her, feeling no sympathy, though.

Miranda picked up on it immediately. "What's the matter? You're as cold as ice," she proclaimed. "Don't you care about what happened to Raine?"

Olivia sat stonily, watching her. All this emotion could certainly be a camouflage and Olivia wasn't going to get caught in it.

"Don't you care?" Miranda repeated.

Olivia had no intention of proclaiming how much she cared. That was why she was here, wasn't it? The way she cared was by being committed to getting the truth of the situation.

"Answer me!" Miranda became more distraught.

"Sure I care," Olivia answered finally, "that's why I'm going to find the killer, fast."

Miranda shuddered. "You're absolutely, positively sure Raine was murdered?"

"Positive," said Olivia. "Raine's head was bashed in with a rock." Olivia wanted to make it as specific and graphic as possible."

Miranda balked. "Has it been confirmed? Do they have a suspect?"

"So far, Victor is a person of interest." Olivia wasn't wasting playing games.

Miranda paled. "I heard that he'd been taken in for questioning," she said in a hushed tone. "I didn't hear anything else."

"And we're all also aware that you and Victor are in a relationship," Olivia said flatly then.

"We had a little fun together, nothing much." Miranda tried to make light of it. "I wouldn't exactly call it a relationship."

"Miranda, this is a homicide investigation now!" Olivia wanted to jar her. "Raine was also involved with Victor, as you know."

"I do know that Raine and Victor were involved." Miranda pulled up to the edge of her seat.

"How long did you know that?" Olivia wasn't letting her off the hook.

"I knew it for a while," Miranda said haltingly. "It was a rumor."

"But you didn't say a thing about it to me when we talked." Olivia stared at her threateningly. "Why didn't you tell me about it then?"

"I didn't tell you because I didn't want to spread gossip," Miranda went on. "I couldn't say exactly what was going on between them. Nobody could."

"You didn't tell me because you were hiding the fact that you were sleeping with Victor as well!" Olivia felt the rage grow within her.

"Listen, what is this? You're acting like I'm the one under investigation." Miranda was growing more anxious by the minute.

"You are," Olivia answered sharply.

"What?" Miranda's voice became shrill. "I'm not in a relationship with Victor! I hang out with him at times."

"Did Raine know about it?" Olivia zoned in.

"I don't know, I have no idea." Miranda's teeth began chattering.

"Don't lie to me!" Olivia stood up. "Raine is dead and most likely Victor killed her. And you're standing square in the middle of all this."

Miranda shot up as well. "Victor didn't kill her. He couldn't have. Under all his bluff, he's a gentle guy."

Olivia laughed.

"You only see his gruff outside," Miranda exclaimed. "But I know him better."

"How did you feel about the fact that your close friend Raine was also having an affair with this gentle guy of yours?" Olivia took it in another direction.

"How far could their affair go?" Miranda became irate. "Raine was married. She was playing with him and Victor knew it! He was only a toy for her."

"Raine had a lot of toys, didn't she?" snapped Olivia.

"Yes, she did." Miranda grew heated then. "Whichever ones she wanted."

Olivia wanted to shake Miranda and wake her up. "Listen, Miranda, Victor was seen up in Miami the day after he left Raine in Key Largo."

Miranda blanched. "Seen by who?"

"It doesn't matter by who!" Olivia was adamant. "He was at the casino. What was he doing there?"

"I have no idea." Miranda shrugged violently, as if tossing the information away.

"You'd better tell me!" Olivia was relentless.

"I don't know, please believe me!"

"Why should I believe you?"

"Why shouldn't you?" Miranda's eyes filled with tears.

"Because my friend is dead," Olivia snapped. "Her head was smashed in by a rock. And if you don't tell me everything you know, you'll be an accessory to the crime. They'll take you in next."

Miranda began trembling. "What are you talking about? How can that be?"

"You're close to Victor and you know more than you're letting on. That makes you an accessory."

Miranda's head hung then.

"If you tell me every single thing you know, completely cooperate, it'll go better for you. You won't be implicated," Olivia continued.

"Implicated?" Miranda seemed unable to believe this.

"If you don't talk, you're obstructing an investigation." Olivia stared at her fiercely. "That's a crime, in case you didn't know."

"Okay, okay." Miranda raised her hands over her face, then put them down and faced Olivia. "I knew that Victor was up in Miami the next day. He came up to see me," Miranda practically gasped.

Olivia was shaken. Had Victor and Miranda plotted this out together? "He came to see you the day after Raine was killed?"

"Victor had no idea she was killed." Miranda spoke under the heat of great pressure. "He told me that he went down to Key Largo with Raine to end the relationship, say good-bye. He was going to tell her it was over and then come up and spend time with me!" She stared straight ahead of her as she spoke.

"Victor planned to say good-bye to Raine? How? By killing her?" Olivia was aghast.

"That's crazy and ridiculous," Miranda shot back. "He just planned to end his relationship with her so we could really be together."

"You'll testify to that under oath?" Olivia asked.

"Of course I will, it's what he told me."

"But you don't know what happened then, do you?" Olivia plunged on. "Raine might not have taken so well to the idea of his saying good-bye. No woman likes to be discarded. They could have fought again."

"Anything could have happened," Miranda flung back.

"Did you help him with this?" Olivia had to ask.

"How could I help him?" Miranda's face grew twisted with fear. "What could I have done?"

"Why was Victor at the casino then when he came to Miami?" Olivia wanted every piece of information.

"He went there often." Miranda could barely speak now. "He knew people there, played the tables."

"Victor went there to gamble the day after Raine went missing?"

"He didn't know she was missing then," Miranda repeated, trying to protect him.

"Or, did he go to pick up money that was due Raine?" Olivia's mind was spinning.

"You're spinning webs." Miranda was breathless. "I just know Victor went down to Key Largo with Raine to break up with her. Then he was coming to see me! We were going to be together forever! I have no idea what he picked up at the casino."

"That should do it," Olivia remarked.

"Do what?" Miranda was horrified.

"That should help us to lock Victor up and throw away the key," said Olivia.

Miranda swung around then as if to flee, but Olivia rushed over and grabbed her.

"You're not going anywhere yet." Olivia detained her.

"You said I would be off the hook if I told you all I knew, though." Miranda looked truly frightened.

"You're off the hook, but you have to give sworn testimony," said Olivia, as she suddenly saw Sean walking toward them.

"Oh, here you guys are," said Sean, nervously. "I've been looking for both of you. "Nessa's here and she wants to talk to Miranda. Abby's here too, and Sloane." Sean was rattling names off as though he were describing a guest list at a formal party. "The pastor has also arrived."

"How about your parents?" Miranda turned to Sean.

"I told you, they're out of the country," Sean replied, in a monotone. "But I'm surrounded by friends and well-wishers."

"That's right, you told me. I forgot," said Miranda.

Why did Sean tell Miranda that? Olivia wondered. When did they have a chance to talk?

"What are you two doing on this patio?" Sean asked then, looking around.

"The investigation has heated up," Olivia plainly reported.

"But they found Raine, didn't they?" Sean said in a suddenly mournful tone. "It's over, isn't it?"

"It's not over, it's only beginning." Olivia had to pierce through the fog that seemed to be surrounding him. "It's the beginning of the search for the killer."

At that moment, Olivia saw Edward approaching. He was walking toward them, wagging his finger and shaking his head, as if it were doomsday and he was giving them all a fierce warning to beware.

CHAPTER TWENTY FOUR

Olivia caught up with Wayne in front of the hotel, immediately after Sean and Edward insisted upon leaving with Miranda.

"Okay, let's walk at the beach," Wayne said, "and fill each other in."

Olivia was glad to get away from the noise and crowds that had descended upon the hotel. She and Wayne walked a short distance to the small beach that Raine had last been seen at. Fortunately, the day had grown a little cooler, with odd, turbulent winds sweeping the Keys.

"You go first," said Wayne as they got to the water's edge.

"I feel like I'm walking in Raine's footsteps," Olivia murmured, uneasily.

"No, you're walking on solid ground," Wayne replied immediately. "You're safe, you're protected."

"I couldn't have done this without your support," Olivia replied then, realizing how important it was to have a partner while investigating a crime.

"Thank you," said Wayne. "You've been a big support too."

"How's it going with Lorna?" Olivia couldn't help ask, suddenly realizing that Wayne hadn't mentioned her for the longest while.

"It's not going at all." Wayne looked away. "We've decided to call it quits."

Olivia was startled. "I'm so sorry."

"Nothing to be sorry about. It was a hard choice, but it's better this way," said Wayne. "There are too many important points on which we do not converge. We never have and never will. At this point, we're getting in each other's way."

Olivia wanted to ask more questions, but also wanted to preserve Wayne's privacy. He would tell her what he wanted, when he could, she thought.

"That's rough," said Olivia. "It's a loss."

"Yes, it is," Wayne responded. "I haven't been assigned someone new yet. It'll happen soon. Right now Raine is tops on everyone's mind."

"I'm glad she is," said Olivia.

"So am I," Wayne agreed. "Now tell me what Miranda had to say."

"She said Victor went down to Key Largo to break up with Raine," Olivia spoke quickly. "Victor told her that after they broke up, he and Miranda could really be together."

"My God," Wayne scoffed. "I've heard that song before. It's doubtful Victor can be with anyone for long. We've checked him out. The guy's basically a loner who attracts women like flies and gets a kick out of it. Then he gets sick of them and moves on to the next. He works alone with a woodworking business out of his house. His neighbors say they see him walking around alone late at night a lot, whistling strange tunes."

"Not a reassuring picture," said Olivia.

"But it's also great to find out that his intention was to get rid of Raine on the spot," Wayne added. "Adds fuel to the fire."

"I'd say his intention was to get rid of her one way or another," breathed Olivia.

"Exactly," Wayne agreed. "This goes to motive. Miranda has to testify under oath, you know."

"She will," said Olivia. "I turned up the heat and threatened her."

"Why was that was necessary?" Wayne was surprised.

"At first she tried to act casual about it, as if her relationship with Victor didn't mean much," Olivia reported.

"It doesn't," Wayne assured Olivia. "Miranda may think it does, but she's in fantasy land. Anyway, this information helps to round out the picture. I'm going to call it in to the station now."

"Wait." For no reason at all, Olivia felt apprehensive. "What's the rest of the picture? Fill me in first."

"Okay," Wayne agreed. "Forensics have assured us that it's definite that Raine was brutally murdered. There's no question about that now. At first they thought the blow to the head could have been a result of being tossed around for days in the water. But now they have definite evidence that the blow was personally inflicted."

"Whew," said Olivia, fascinated to see things coming together on their own. "Do they think Victor killed her and then drowned her?"

"Looks like it," said Wayne. "We also found a guest who had a room next to theirs in the hotel. The guest reported that he heard Victor and Raine arguing pretty heatedly late that afternoon. Now you tell me that Miranda said he was coming down here to get rid of her. It's all adding up."

Olivia felt an enormous sense of sadness come over her. "It is," she had to admit. "How about Victor's being sighted in the casino in Miami? How does that fit in?"

"Yeah, that too," said Wayne. "My sources tell me Victor picked up something Dupris had left for Raine. She called the casino earlier to tell them to give it to him."

Olivia shook her head slowly. "That's a nail in his coffin."

"That and everything else," Wayne replied. "Sounds like everything he did was premeditated. He knew about the package. He's planned out his every move, step by step."

"Why did he do it? For money?" asked Olivia.

"There's tons of reasons why someone actually kills," Wayne murmured.

"Could Victor be working for Dupris?" Olivia suggested.

"There's no evidence of that, and we've checked it out," Wayne replied quickly. "Dupris was actually located, he's off partying with someone else."

Olivia smiled. "Do you think Miranda was involved in Raine's disappearance?" Olivia asked then.

"I don't," Wayne answered. "I think she's just another lonely woman who got pulled in way over her head."

Olivia shuddered then thinking of how the same thing had happened to her with Todd.

"What does Sean say about it all?" Olivia couldn't help asking.

"I don't know," said Wayne. "I haven't spoken much to him yet. He's surrounded by Raine's friends. And this pastor, who's like a father to him."

"I'm glad he has that at least," said Raine.

"So am I," said Wayne. "Listen, I've got to call your piece of information in to the station now. You've done a wonderful job. We're proud of you."

The words were good to hear, but at the same time, hollow. Raine was gone; Olivia hadn't been able to bring her home.

"I wish it had turned out differently," Olivia said.

Wayne stopped and gave her a long glance. "So do I," he said, "so do we all. But at least it looks as though we have the killer. Let me call the station and tell them what you've found."

Wayne picked up his phone then to put in the call. "Wayne here," he started, "more news on the case."

Then he stopped speaking abruptly. "Yeah, go ahead, tell me," Wayne said, listening intently to every word on the other end.

"Okay, that does it," Wayne said finally. "There's no question about it then! Sure, I'll call you back in a few minutes with what we've got to add."

"What was that?" Olivia moved closer to him.

"More hard evidence, finally," Wayne reported. "They've checked the amount of time Raine's body was in the water. There's absolutely no question she was definitely killed the night she and Wayne were swimming here."

"My God," breathed Olivia.

Wayne looked at her. "It's Victor. Case closed."

"Closed?" Olivia could barely believe it.

"Why don't you go find Sean now and tell him?" Wayne suggested. "I'll call in information about what Miranda told you and then we can tie things up."

*

By the time Olivia found Sean with Raine's friends out on the hotel veranda they'd already heard the latest reports. Sean stood up from his seat to greet Olivia with an outstretched hand.

"You've done a great job," he said, a pleased look on his face.

"Thank you," said Olivia, surprised Sean was still standing. A tall man with pepper and salt hair who must have been Sean's pastor stood up as well as Olivia approached. Miranda, Sloane, and Nessa also sat there, looking forlorn.

"Pleased and proud to meet you, Olivia," the pastor exclaimed. "Despite her recent fall from grace, Raine was a fine woman, and I do hope we will all remember her that way."

Sean nodded somberly as the pastor spoke.

"We all can be victims of sin and confusion in this painful, temporary world," the pastor continued.

Olivia was struck by the pastor's bearing and, to her surprise, found comfort herself in his strong words.

"Thank you for being here to support Sean," Olivia responded.

"Of course, of course," the pastor exclaimed. "Sean has my support eternally. He is a pillar of our community. Sean is the victim of a terrible deed, and we will all stand behind him strongly."

The pastor then gave Olivia a long glance. "You have helped Sean a great deal and we appreciate you," he said carefully.

Olivia felt his iron of will. She also felt the strength Sean was taking from him and also from the sympathy of Raine's friends. Olivia wondered where Edward was and how he was doing. She was also struck that no one had mentioned Raine's mother or daughter back home.

"How's the rest of the family doing, Sean?" Olivia asked.

Sean looked at Olivia then with a cool eye. "My true family is right here around me now," he replied.

Everyone grew still.

"You understand what Sean is saying, I'm sure." The pastor stepped in for him. "He's referring to the famous saying: 'We're born in one family, but we don't die in the same family.' It simply means that you draw those meant to be close to you as you go through your life journey. Raine was given to Sean for a short while. He will not be bereft now that she has departed. His true family has gathered for him here."

The pastor's words alarmed Olivia. She wondered if she was included in Sean's true family now. It was a strange thought. Olivia also wondered momentarily who her true family really was.

In a few moments Wayne joined the group to briskly confirm that law enforcement had enough evidence now to convict Victor. The case was closed.

Sighs of relief rose all around, especially from Raine's friends. Olivia knew she should feel relieved as well, but a heaviness fell upon her heart like a rock. Something didn't sit well with her, though she had no idea what in the world it was.

CHAPTER TWENTY FIVE

Once back in Miami, the first thing Olivia wanted to do after checking into her hotel was to go speak to Sean. He had told her to come to see him quickly, to pick up the check he had for her. Where would she go then? For a moment Olivia felt unmoored. She'd left the life she'd had behind, and had no idea what was waiting for her now.

Wayne told her not to, to give it some time. Sean needed to unwind. But something was tugging at her. Olivia felt she had to go now. She wanted to be ready to leave Miami right after the funeral. There was a lot she also had to process, as well as everyone else.

"Where will you be going after the funeral?" Wayne had asked.

"I don't know, I'm not sure," said Olivia.

"Don't rush away," Wayne responded. "Stay down in Miami awhile, why don't you?"

But Olivia didn't want to. "I don't think so," she said. There was nothing in Miami that held her. The case was over. She needed to keep working and she knew it, but was entirely unsure what that would look like now. Olivia didn't say that to Wayne, though.

"Do you plan to go home and visit your parents?" Wayne sounded concerned.

"I don't have plans at the moment," Olivia replied, "but I do feel I need to speak to Sean and tie things up."

Wayne nodded. "Why?"

Olivia didn't know why, but deep down she was not totally at ease with Victor's guilt. It had all lined up too neatly for her taste.

"There are unanswered questions lingering in my mind," she then said to Wayne. "I want Sean to fill me in on the answers."

"Questions about Miranda?" asked Wayne, surprised.

"Miranda and also Sloane," replied Olivia. "I also still want to know exactly what was in the package Victor picked up at the casino."

"It was obviously money," said Wayne. "And how would Sean even know? Law enforcement will have all the details shortly, anyway. You don't have to go."

"But I want to," Olivia objected.

Wayne simply nodded. "If you have to speak to Sean right away, you have to. But remember, the case is closed."

Open or closed, Olivia knew she wouldn't feel complete until all the questions in her mind were answered. She needed to feel that she'd done her job thoroughly.

"I heard that Sean's going to spend some time at a hideaway he and Raine have, before the funeral," Wayne offered. "Then he'll return home. Why not wait and see him afterwards?"

That wasn't even a possibility. Olivia felt even more strongly that she needed to see him now.

"Can you give me the address of the hideaway, please?" she requested.

"Of course," said Wayne, "and if you're going, please take this along." Wayne slipped a little recorder into Olivia's hand. "It never hurts to have everything said on record. Especially when you appear somewhere uninvited. People don't like that. They can accuse you of all kinds of things."

*

A thousand thoughts rushed through Olivia's mind as she made her way down to the hideaway that Sean was staying at. How could he go there alone without Raine now? Wouldn't it bring up too many memories? The road leading to Sean's hideaway was practically empty at this time of day and Olivia was relieved. She realized how deeply exhausted she felt, how hard it would have been now battling traffic. And what had become of Edward? Olivia wondered as she drove down a steep hill toward the edge of a pond.

When Olivia arrived at Sean's getaway, she parked near the road, got out, and walked carefully down another sloping hill. It suddenly struck her that she probably should have called before she arrived. But Sean had told her to come and pick up her check several times. She was following his instructions. Olivia wondered briefly then if he would be alone. The idea that someone else might be there had never occurred to her. And it was startling.

Olivia walked up to the front door, knocked hard on it, and waited a few moments. No answer. She knocked again. Still no answer. Sean was probably down at the pond, reflecting, or walking or just sitting on the grass.

On the off chance that the door was open, Olivia turned the knob. To her surprise the door opened easily and she walked in.

The getaway was small, but artfully decorated, with antique pieces and lace curtains blowing in the breeze over the open windows. Olivia stood silently, looking around, remembering everything about her friend. This place seemed to be a testimony to her. Raine's colorful touches and photographs were everywhere. They tugged at Olivia's heart. .

"You just walked in?" Olivia suddenly heard Sean's deep voice behind her.

Olivia turned to see him standing there in jeans, his hair messy, as if he'd just returned from the outdoors.

"I tried knocking," Olivia began to excuse herself.

"No, it's fine. You're here." Sean walked toward her. "You did a good job, Olivia, I told you that already."

"Yes, thank you," Olivia remarked as she heard a rustle in the next room. "Is somebody here?" she asked Sean, startled.

Sean immediately bypassed her question. "What did you come here for? To collect your check?"

"Yes, that's right," said Olivia, thinking that was the best reply. "You told me to."

"I told you to collect your check, not come here uninvited to visit. Okay, go out on the patio there, and I'll prepare it for you," Sean said, in a strange tone.

"I can wait in here," Olivia answered.

"No, go out there if you don't mind," he ordered.

Put out, Olivia stepped onto the patio, wondering why Sean didn't want her in the house. It definitely seemed possible that someone was in there with him. Most likely he didn't want Olivia seeing who it was. Her mind started racing. Was it Sloane? Or possibly Miranda even? Olivia had been bothered by both of them. Sloane had definitely started trying to get too close to Sean the minute Raine disappeared. And Miranda couldn't be trusted. Olivia recalled Sean mentioning something personal about his family to Miranda, even. It had struck Olivia as odd then, and came back to her vividly now.

Olivia wanted to turn and go back into the house despite Sean's instructions. There was no reason she should stand out here alone, wait for payment, and then drive away. After all the work she'd put in, if someone was inside with him, Olivia had a right to know who it was. And why.

Olivia walked back into the house and stood tentatively in the main room almost the same moment Sean entered as well.

"I thought I told you to wait outside." He looked displeased.

"It's cold out there," said Olivia.

"No, it isn't." Sean's voice grew harsh. "Why are you here? What do you want of me?"

Olivia knew that he had to be feeling edgy, but she'd never heard him speak this way to her before.

"Is someone here with you?" Olivia repeated, nonplussed. If Sean was hiding something, she had to know what.

"I beg your pardon? Last time I looked, I didn't hire you to investigate me, did I?" Sean barked.

"I'm not investigating you, I'm just asking a question." Olivia's heart started to pound.

"It's none of your business if someone is here with me or not." Sean glared at her.

"But you've made it my business, Sean," Olivia responded. "Is Miranda here with you?"

At that, Sean's hands clenched and his eyes opened wide. "How dare you?" he shouted. "Who the hell do you think you are, anyway? You keep going on like this and I'll rip up the check."

Olivia was outraged by his comment. "Rip it up all you want," she flung back. "I would still do this even if I wasn't paid a cent. I'm doing it for Raine."

Sean's jaw clenched.

"And I have other questions, too!" Olivia's voice grew louder as her resolve grew. "What package did Victor pick up at the casino? I heard the package was supposed to be for Raine."

Sean stamped his foot hard on the floor. "You heard, you heard, what the hell do you know? Why are you asking me?"

"Why did Victor pick up the package?" Olivia asked swiftly. Sean had said that he'd paid all of Raine's gambling debts. Why wouldn't he know what was in the package?

"How the hell do I know?" Sean looked furious. "Raine probably told him to do it for her. And I'm glad she did. It gave us a trail straight to Victor."

A strange thought hit Olivia intensely then. It gave them a straight trail to the one who paid Raine's gambling debts, she thought. Could it have been Sean?

Sean closed his eyes slowly, stood there, and didn't move, as the noise in the next room grew louder.

Olivia felt herself break into a sweat. "Who's in the next room?" she pushed harder, wanting for Sean's facade to crack. There was more to the story, Olivia was positive now.

"Get the hell out of here." Sean came toward Olivia slowly, as if he were about to push her out the door.

"Stop it, Sean, stop it." Pastor Harris suddenly entered from the next room. "In the name of God, calm down!"

"I can't calm down anymore and I won't." Sean turned to the pastor now. "I've taken too much for too long."

"You will and you can," Pastor Harris assured him. "And I also want you to tell Olivia the truth about everything you know. Olivia needs it. Everyone does."

"The truth, the truth!" Sean became frantic. "Please get out of here now and take a walk," he said to the pastor. "I'll tell Olivia the complete truth if you'll leave us alone."

"Agreed," said the pastor as he then flipped around and walked out of the house down a thin back lane.

Olivia was trembling as Sean turned back to her. "What truth?" she asked breathlessly.

"The truth is that Raine deserved everything that happened." Sean's voice became stranger as he spoke. "Nobody knows what I went through with her! And I was the one who paid all her gambling debts."

Olivia was stunned. "You? Why didn't you tell anybody that?"

Sean's face grew red. "The pastor knows it!"

"How about law enforcement?" demanded Olivia.

"Enough was enough," Sean thundered. "I didn't want to be implicated in Raine's sins! I told Pastor Harris that too, but he said she was my wife and I had no choice about it. Raine bled me for money, it didn't stop. Edward refused to help out."

"Raine's condition was worsening and you knew it," Olivia shot back.

"And it wasn't only the gambling," Sean went on. "She couldn't even be a mother."

"She needed help," Olivia cried out.

"She needed to be punished," Sean growled. "It was one thing after another. I knew about Victor all along. That's how she thanked me! By cheating on me right under my nose. Raine went from bad to worse and nothing could stop her!" Sean bared his teeth.

"She needed help, Sean," Olivia gasped again.

"She wouldn't take it, though, no matter what I did." Sean suddenly looked completely helpless. "I tried and tried and so did the pastor. Nothing worked. So she finally got what she deserved."

"No one deserves to die!" Olivia felt a wave of horror.

"Raine did," Sean suddenly insisted. "Stop looking at me that way!" Sean lunged over to Olivia. "I tried to keep my awful life with Raine quiet for as long as I could. I begged her to straighten up, go to Pastor Harris to help her, and at the end, she laughed right in our faces."

Suddenly the pieces were falling together in front of Olivia's eyes.

"All the time you made it look like it was Victor, didn't you?" Olivia quickly got it. "He was the perfect foil. You set him up to look guilty as hell. Including his picking up a package at the casino meant for Raine."

Sean stopped on a dime.

"You even pulled Miranda into it, didn't you?" Olivia went on breathlessly. "Her friends were plenty jealous of her. This could have been paradise for them. You got Miranda to get between Raine and Victor."

Sean reddened.

"Did you try to make Miranda feel sorry for you?" Olivia went on. "Did you tell her if she broke up Raine and Victor it would help save your marriage?"

Sean laughed loudly. "That part was easy. What I didn't expect was that Miranda and Victor would actually fall for each other. There's no end to the stupidity of women."

"You're the fool," Olivia hissed.

"Look at that." Sean took a step closer. "Now you've turned on me, just like Raine did. One after another. But I can't let that happen again, can I? I did what I had to, to save all of us."

"You did what?" Olivia trembled.

"Three guesses." Sean smiled oddly. "You're on a roll, keep going!"

"You killed Raine?" Olivia trembled. "You?"

"And it looks like you're next," Sean growled. "And no one will ever know what happened to you, either. Basically, they won't even care. You made a mistake, Olivia!"

"I made the mistake?" Olivia was suddenly filled with loathing.

"I hired you to cover up for me and make me look good! Not to take me down," thundered Sean.

"You hired me to make it look like a real investigation was going on!" Olivia exclaimed. "Does Pastor Harris know that you killed Raine?"

"Nobody knows," Sean growled. "Except you. And how can I let you live after you know that?"

Sean edged over to small, wooden table on top of which sat a huge, craggy rock. In one fell swoop, he leaned over and grabbed it.

"Put the rock down!" Olivia took charge. "You don't know what you're doing! You'll never get away with it. Everything will point to you!"

Sean grinned. "I know just what I'm doing. And I knew what I was doing then. You girls think I'm a dunce, well, think again."

Olivia began to feel alarmed. "I never thought you were a dunce. I thought you were a good person."

"I am a good person," Sean thundered again. "Raine was the monster, not me. She had it coming for a long time. And I'm not only good, I'm smart. I knew she was going to Key Largo with

Victor that night and I went down the same time. Then I waited for exactly the right moment. When they were swimming that night, I hid in the bushes, watched and waited."

Olivia shuddered. "Like a crazed animal."

"At first they were swimming, but then they started fighting," Sean continued. "I was thrilled, delighted! It made me happy. Raine was yelling at him for all she was worth and finally Victor had enough. He ran out of the ocean telling her to go to hell and flew away on the beach. I ran right in then, ready to send her to hell myself. First I grabbed the big rock I brought with me. Then I charged into the water, splashing for all I was worth. At first Raine thought it was Victor returning. It wasn't, though, it was me. When she saw my face close up to hers, she started yelling like a wild bird trapped in a net. Trapped, she was trapped, and I was happy for it."

Olivia's heart pounded as he spoke.

"It's me, it's Sean, and I'm nobody's fool, I yelled right in her face. Then I raised the rock and hit her hard. It was quick, it was easy. She deserved what she got. I was freeing the world and myself from her sins. The pastor told me when the vermin are cleared away you make a space for something good to come. I was cleaning the vermin! Raine deserved to die. And now you do, too!"

As Sean stared into Olivia's eyes, she felt a huge, dark cloud descending over both of them.

"Wayne knows that I'm here." Olivia's voice trembled. "If I don't return he'll come searching for me!"

Sean laughed again and grabbed Olivia's shoulder with his free hand.

"Nobody will search for you because you don't mean a thing to them," he barked.

Thankfully, Olivia heard the sound of a rustle again, this time right outside the front door.

"Help!" she started shouting, hoping the pastor was returning.

Sean grasped Olivia's neck then, enjoying every ounce of fear that was racing through her. But she wasn't going to die. She refused to. The rustling noise got louder.

"What's that? Do you hear that?" Olivia barely managed to speak as Sean held the rock directly over her head now.

"In a moment it will be as if you never lived at all," he whispered. "Take a minute to think about that, Olivia. All your stupid plans will die down. Your crazy eyes will stop flashing. Your body will fall limp on the ground. Your life will amount to nothing at all. Like Raine's!"

"Pastor!" Olivia summoned her strength and managed to cry out, as the front door suddenly burst open.

To Olivia's total amazement, Wayne and another officer charged in with their revolvers out, pointed.

"Give me that rock immediately or you're dead on the spot," Wayne shouted as Sean stood there, horrified.

The other officer ran over, grabbed Sean, and pulled the rock from him. Then he yanked Sean's arms behind his back.

"You can't take me in for anything," Sean started mumbling. "Olivia's alive, she's unharmed."

"We have every word you said on tape," Wayne shot back. "I slipped a recorder into Olivia's pocket before she left."

Sean's face grew dark as suddenly the pastor walked back up into the house again.

"I thought I heard someone calling for me," the pastor declared. "Do you need me, Sean? Is something wrong?"

"He doesn't need you for anything anymore," Wayne replied for him. "Say good-bye to him now. It's way too late for your golden-haired boy."

The officer pushed Sean to the side and, finally able to move, Olivia fled from his side.

Both Olivia and Wayne ran straight to each other then, as he pulled her to him in a long, comforting embrace. Olivia had forgotten how wonderful it could be to be held like that. How strengthening and healing.

"My God, my God," Wayne murmured. "Thank God we got here in time. Thank God you're okay, Olivia. I don't know what I would have ever done if something happened to you."

CHAPTER TWENTY SIX

In what seemed like a matter of moments the news flashed everywhere.

Olivia Wells bravely hunts down the real killer. Raine's death is finally solved. Victor to be let out of jail.

The commotion and shock the news caused could not be contained. Over and over the announcers mentioned what a fine citizen Sean had been. How he must have gone temporarily insane when he discovered his wife's infidelity. They also mentioned the uncanny bravery and insight that Olivia had displayed.

Wayne would not leave Olivia's side though, now. "You've been through an ordeal," he kept saying. "You need time off to take care of yourself."

Olivia appreciated his concern greatly. "Time off?" She finally smiled. "I left my job at home, remember? Right now I'm unemployed. I have all the time in the world."

"Of course I remember," Wayne replied. "But you need time down here to just relax, hang out at the beach, take walks in town."

The idea sounded good to Olivia. Where else would she go now? The last place she wanted to return to was the city.

"And I have more to say when you're ready, too." Wayne's voice lowered.

"I'm ready now," said Olivia, curious. "What is it? Tell me."

Wayne smiled. "I've had a few calls from Chief Tan since all of this happened." Wayne paused nervously. "There was a lot we had to discuss."

"Yes?" Olivia was curious. She wondered why Wayne was speaking in such a halting tone. It wasn't like him. Whatever he had to say seemed very important.

"Chief Tan said the force is ready to offer you a job, if you enter the academy and get licensed," Wayne finally burst out. "We've got more cases down here than we can handle and you're top notch!"

Olivia was startled. "A job for me as a detective?" It was the last thing she expected to hear.

"A job as my partner," Wayne added emphatically. "You're such a wonderful addition to the force and we work so well together. You can get whatever extra training you need on the job."

Olivia felt a long chill. She loved the idea of being Wayne's partner, but it was also a huge change in lifestyle. She'd have to move down to the Keys, give up her apartment in the city.

Wayne turned to her directly, suddenly looking boyish. "Are you up for it?" he asked hopefully. "It's fantastic work. There's never a boring day. You learn a tremendous amount and help lots of people."

Olivia looked at the sudden twinkle in his eyes. A sense of excitement and purpose flooded her. She had no idea if she was up for it, but she knew this was a unique opportunity. It wouldn't come again. And she would definitely regret it if she passed it by.

"Yes," Olivia said suddenly, from out of nowhere.

Wayne grinned.

"Okay, let's go to the station now and work out the details."

She walked with him, and as she did, slowly she felt that old feeling returning, welling up within her: hope. Before her, she suddenly felt, awaited a whole new life.

COMING SOON!

Book #3 in the MURDER IN THE KEYS series!

About Jaden Skye

#1 bestselling author Jaden Skye is author of the bestselling romantic suspense series CARIBBEAN MURDER, which includes 16 books (and counting), and which begins with DEATH BY HONEYMOON (Book #1).

Jaden is also author of the romance series A PERFECT STRANGER.

Jaden is also author of the new romantic suspense series MURDER IN THE KEYS, which begins with NO PLACE TO DIE (Book #1).

Jaden has always been fascinated with mystery, wrongful death, lies, deception and the power of the truth to prevail. Her romantic suspense/mystery novels feature strong female protagonists who must overcome insurmountable obstacles, and through them, she seeks to get to the very heart of the nature of justice and love. Please visit www.jadenskye.com to find links to stay in touch with Jaden via Facebook, Twitter, Goodreads, her blog, and a whole bunch of other places. Jaden loves to hear from you, so don't be shy and check back often!

Books by Jaden Skye

THE CARIBBEAN MURDER SERIES
DEATH BY HONEYMOON (Book #1)
DEATH BY DIVORCE (Book #2)
DEATH BY MARRIAGE (Book #3)
DEATH BY DESIRE (Book #4)
DEATH BY DECEIT (Book #5)
DEATH BY JEALOUSY (Book #6)
DEATH BY PROPOSAL (Book #7)
DEATH BY OBSESSION (Book #8)
DEATH BY DEVOTION (Book #9)
DEATH BY BETRAYAL (Book #10)
DEATH BY REQUEST (Book #11)
DEATH BY ENGAGEMENT (Book #12)
DEATH BY SEDUCTION (Book #13)
DEATH BY TEMPTATION (Book #14)
DEATH BY INVITATION (Book #15)
DEATH BY WEDDING (Book #16)

THE TOM'S RIVER SAGA
A PERFECT STRANGER (Book #1)

MURDER IN THE KEYS
NO PLACE TO DIE (Book #1)
NO PLACE TO VANISH (Book #2)

THE KILLING GAME
INVITATION TO DIE (Book #1)
INVITATION TO MADNESS (Book #2)
INVITATION TO AGONY (Book #3)

67533372R00096